The Colony:

A Political Tale

REGGIE RIVERS

To Scott -
Best Wishes!

Reggie Rivers

Book design by MacGraphics Services
Cover design and illustration by
Marty Petersen Artwork & Design

The book is a novel. References to real people, events,
establishments, organizations, or locales are intended only to provide a
sense of authenticity, and are used fictitiously. All other characters, and
all incidents of dialogue, are drawn from the author's imagination and
are not to be construed as real.

Published by
SCA Publishing
16 Inverness Place East, Suite E-200
Englewood, CO 80112
(303) 790-2020
www.SharonCooper.com

Distributed by Books West

Library of Congress Cataloging-in-Publication Data
Rivers, Reggie
The Colony: A Political Tale / by Reggie Rivers
p. cm
ISBN: 978-0-9704542-3-2
LCCN: 2009931786

Rivers' new novel intrigues the reader from page one and exudes pheromones of required reading. Who knew the best view of our political reality would be seen through the compound eyes of ants? Machiavelli and Orwell would appreciate this one...
　　–James Mejía, Former Member, Denver School Board

If you enjoyed Orwell's Animal Farm, you'll appreciate The Colony. The parallels between the ants quest for food and our country's short-sighted thirst for oil is all too real.
　　–Michael Huttner, Founder & CEO of ProgressNow

A truly poignant, engaging expose' on geo-politics through the insightful eyes of some of nature's most remarkable species. The Colony draws you in with its charismatic cast, enlightens with its unique socio-political metaphor, and delights with its silky storyline. Once you start the journey into The Colony, it commands your attention all the way to its climatic culmination.
　　–Alex Harz, writer/director

Reggie spins a fast paced tale of war, greed, corruption and power which is well-written and interesting. The Colony will leave you with a deeper understanding of policy and struggle through the well thought out and carefully planned ant colony metaphor. A book that will leave you questioning political actions in years to come.
　　–Luke Houghton, Griffith Business School,
　　Griffith University, Brisbane, Australia.

The Colony is the Animal Farm of a new generation. This creative tale of ant colonies as metaphors for the nations of the world and how they interact with each other is a masterpiece that will bring new light on international relations for many.
　　–Rob Doughty, Rob Doughty Communications

For Stephanie and Malik

Acknowledgements

I owe a debt of gratitude to many people for helping me bring this book to fruition. Professors Jim Cole and Alan Gilbert read the first few chapters when the manuscript was only about 30 pages long, and with their encouragement and support, I enrolled at the University of Denver and earned a Master's in Global Studies. Editor Peggy Cole was sensational as always. She followed me deep into the world of ants and helped me stay true to the basic nature of ants, without forgetting that this story was really about humans. I appreciate the Graduate School of International Studies at DU for having the flexibility to allow me to write this allegory as the thesis for my degree. Karen Saunders at MacGraphics Services (www.macgraphics.net) did a wonderful job of overseeing the design of the book. Artist Marty Petersen (www.martyart.com) produced an amazing cover image and interior layout designer Lindsey Hurwitz patiently went through the story with me line by line correcting the final draft. Thank you to Ann Marie Gordon at United Graphics. I appreciate Sharon and Steve Cooper for their continued support for my writing and speaking career. Thank you to my parents, Frankie and Phyllis and my siblings Darryl, Mike, Jackie and Gwen, who all read versions of the manuscript and gave me valuable feedback. And thank you to my wife, Stephanie, and my son, Malik, for the sacrifices that they made while I was in school and working on this book.

The Colony:

A Political Tale

REGGIE RIVERS

one

A wasp, sleek and black, zipped inches above a field of blue and white lupine blossoms, her head swinging from side to side, studying the ground below. Her coppery wings caught the midday sunlight and threw flickering shadows onto the petals of the flowers. Her long, segmented antennae aimed, like daggers, at the earthen dome of Antistan rising in the distance.

Insects looked up toward the low-pitched thumping of the wasp's wings. But she flew by so quickly that no one could positively identify anything other than the thin red lines running along her flanks and the barbed stinger protruding from the tip of her abdomen. She was still eight corons from Antistan—approximately a two-hour walk, a one-hour run, or a twenty-minute flight.

Between her and the hive, a large Alpha Zee soldier sat atop a swaying dandelion, studying the horizon. His square head, twitching antennae and long, serrated mandibles threw a grotesque shadow onto the ground that looked like a prehistoric beast with enormous tusks. He heard the distinct rumble of the wasp's wings and carefully scanned the sky until he spotted her—a zigzagging silhouette against a clear blue backdrop.

A platoon of ants stood below the lookout with their big bodies stacked on top of each other. They held three sunflower plants in their powerful jaws, bracing the plants against the light push of the wind. The lookout emitted a pheromone signal, and the ants below released the stalks. The sunflowers toppled to the ground with a thunderous crash.

The falling flowers—a pre-arranged signal—caught the wasp's attention. She flew toward the newly created clearing and hovered over rows and rows of clay-red army ants staring up at her with dark eyes and gleaming mandibles. She descended in a tight spiral, her wings buzzing faster and louder as she neared the ground. A drop of venom gathered at the tip of her stinger as she landed.

The leader—the largest of the soldiers—marched forward in stiff, precise steps. His chest was wide, and his waist narrow. The chitin of his body armor bore the scars of many battles, and his thick mandibles arched out to threatening points. He stopped in front of the wasp, staring at her contemptuously.

"I'm General Edmund Gant," he said, his voice gravelly. "Leader of the Alpha Zee Army."

The wasp's streamlined frame was three times larger than the General's, but her dark skin was not armored. The ants' mandibles could easily slice through her, and though her stinger was a formidable weapon, it wouldn't help if the soldiers of the Alpha Zee tribe suddenly swarmed her.

"I'm Yasura Hasan," she said quietly.

General Gant fixed her with a steely gaze, as if her name annoyed him.

"It's time to move out," he commanded.

Yasura felt the dangerous undercurrent of ants' rage, and she knew that the slightest provocation could set them off—the sooner she got out of there, the better.

But, still, she had questions. "Where will I find the cocoons?" She glanced up at the sun, which was still high in the sky.

The General sneered, as if her eagerness were a sign of weakness.

"They're located in the northeast quadrant."

"You're sure about the target?" Yasura didn't want to waste

her chemical payload on the wrong mound.

"Our intelligence is rock solid," the General said. "Four caterpillar cocoons."

Four was more than enough.

"And the scent?"

"Gorman!" General Gant barked. "Front and center!" A soldier raced forward, and General Gant indicated different points on Gorman's body. "He's got the colony scent on his mandibles and the smell of larvae at the base of his antennae."

Yasura studied the soldier carefully. To acquire the scent, she'd have to place her head dangerously close to his mandibles. With a quick flick of his jaw, he could snap her in half. Corporal Timothy Gorman smiled mockingly, daring her to lean in.

Yasura Hasan couldn't defeat an entire platoon of ants on the ground, but one-on-one none of them could match her speed or agility. Suddenly, she darted into the air, pin-wheeled 180 degrees and landed on Gorman's back. Her movement was so fluid and so quick that no one had time to react. She drove her stinger into the junction of his trunk and meta-soma—the third section of his body—and Corporal Gorman screamed in pain. The other ants stepped forward, clicking their mandibles rhythmically with hard, angry chops.

"Stand down," General Gant said calmly to his troops. To Yasura he barked, "What the hell are you doing?"

She stood on top of Gorman. "I'm just making sure this soldier doesn't get any funny ideas."

General Gant shook his head. "If you sting him, we'll kill you."

"Oh, I won't waste my poison on him," Yasura said with a wry smile. "If he makes one false move, I'll lay my eggs inside

3

of him, and you'll watch my progeny eat him from the inside over the next few weeks."

The General frowned, losing some of his swagger. Yasura knew that he didn't care about Corporal Gorman's life; he was worried about the eggs. If she discharged them into Gorman's body, the mission would be compromised.

"I should kill you for your impudence," the General growled.

Yasura said, "But you won't."

"You want to bet your life on it?" His face bristled with aggression.

"You need me."

"Barely."

"Barely?" Yasura said, chuckling softly. "Well, I suppose that's true, but I've survived on *barely* for many moons. We both know that you need me."

General Gant rolled his eyes. "We can *always* find another wasp."

"Today?" Yasura asked, grinning. "Pregnant?"

General Gant let out an impatient breath and stared into the distance. "What do you want?"

"I want Corporal Gorman to stand very still while I acquire the scent." She pushed the tip of her stinger a little deeper, and Gorman arched his back, grimacing.

Yasura Hasan lowered her antennae between his mandibles and rubbed back and forth. She did the same at the top of his forelegs.

"*Atta*," the wasp said.

"That's right," General Gant nodded. "Leafcutter ants."

"Piece of cake." She retracted her stinger and flew off Tim Gorman's back, landing next to the General. Gorman groaned and twisted his trunk.

General Gant said, "You'd better do what you're supposed to do."

Yasura said, "No need to worry, General. This mission serves our mutual interests."

"We'll give you air and perimeter support."

Yasura shook her head. "There's no need for a big parade. I do this all the time."

"Not in The Grove you don't."

Yasura thought for a moment. That was true. "So why let me operate here now?"

The General shook his head. He would not answer that question. "How many eggs will you put down?"

Yasura shrugged. "Ten, maybe twelve."

"Good," General Gant said. "There's one other thing." He turned toward the crowd of soldiers. "Hasina, get up here!" A pale, gaunt ant emerged from the platoon of muscled soldiers and hurried up to General Gant's side. "You'll take her with you," he ordered.

Yasura Hasan looked at the pitifully small ant in front of her and wondered when the Alpha Zee military had adopted a mascot. She glanced at General Gant, thinking this must be a joke, but his face was serious. Yasura brought her attention back to the tiny ant, who looked at her with lazy indifference. Hasina had tiny mandibles, so she wasn't a worker or a soldier, but she didn't look like a caretaker either. The truth was that she didn't look like much of anything. Yasura Hasan could not imagine what the Alpha Zee hoped to achieve by delivering this puny ant into Antistan. Yasura lowered her antennae to take a sniff. She didn't recognize the species.

"Who is she?" Yasura asked.

"No one—" The General stopped talking and stared up at the sky. A low rumble grew louder as a bumblebee drew near the clearing. The bee suddenly noticed the rows of soldiers below him and knew that he was in trouble. He sped away as quickly as his tiny wings would carry him.

"Thompson! Anderson!" General Gant ordered.

Two winged males leaped into the sky, their mandibles hinged open. They quickly overtook the ponderous bumblebee and ripped him apart. His dismembered body fell to the ground.

"No witnesses," General Gant said, flaunting the most grotesque smile Yasura had ever seen. She wondered if Alpha Zee flyers would try to kill *her* when she completed her mission. She knew that the ants couldn't keep pace with her in the air. The trick would be to get airborne before they attacked.

"Ready?" General Gant said.

"Yes," Yasura said.

Hasina climbed onto Yasura's back; the little ant's concave body and suction-cup feet conformed perfectly to the wasp's frame.

General Gant turned to his soldiers. "Airborne, load up and lead! Infantry, set up a perimeter! No one gets *into* Antistan, no one gets *out*." He turned back to Yasura. "We'll do two bombing runs. After that, it's all yours."

Twenty-four winged ants rose into the sky, laboring under the weight of rocks cradled in their legs. They zoomed over the flowers in tight formation as ground troops raced through the tall grass.

Yasura Hasan turned her head to look at the ant clinging to her back. "What's your name again?"

"Hasina Binsaw," the little ant said.

"Are you a caretaker?"

"No."

"You're certainly not a worker or a soldier."

"Correct."

"So what are you?"

"I'm a queen."

Yasura craned her neck. She had seen only two queens in her lifetime; neither of them had looked anything like Hasina. "You don't have a big belly."

"Not yet," Hasina said.

Yasura didn't know what to make of that comment. "So what are you going to do in Antistan?"

"I'm going to live there."

Yasura grunted. It sounded like suicide.

two

Yasura Hasan hovered at the edge of the clearing and watched as the Alpha Zee infantry arranged themselves in a huge circle, alternately facing toward and away from the Antistani mound. The airborne forces broke into two groups, attacking from the east and west, releasing their rocks as they dove toward the colony. The rocks, which had been doused with formic acid, hit with a staccato *thump-thump-thump*. They tore deep into the mound, ripping through tunnels and chambers. The bombs instantly killed some ants and trapped thousands more below the surface, where they breathed in fumes of the formic acid and died slowly.

Yasura Hasan waited a few seconds, and then flew to the mound. She knew that her mission was possible solely because all ants identified their siblings and cousins by pheromones—not by appearance. So they were vulnerable to having their pheromones exploited by outsiders. Caterpillars began their metamorphosis outside the mound, where their cocoons emitted a scent identical to that of leafcutter ant larvae. Instinct drove the ants to pick up the caterpillar cocoons and take them into the mound where the alien larvae were carefully tended as if they were ant larvae.

As soon as Yasura Hasan landed on the surface of Antistan, a platoon of soldiers raced toward her in attack formation. They expected Yasura to take flight, but she stood still and calmly pumped a special chemical from her scent glands. The powerful scent stopped the closest ants as forcefully as if they'd run into a wall. The scent also neutralized the ants' colonial pheromone and camouflaged them with the acrid scent of a foreign army. The second wave of Antistani soldiers, deceived by the enemy scent, attacked the first wave of soldiers.

Every ant that came close to Yasura turned into an enemy of Antistan. The colony plunged into a catastrophic pseudo civil war, while Yasura Hasan walked, unmolested, into the mound.

In a darkened chamber deep below the surface, Yasura Hasan found the caterpillar cocoons. She climbed on top of them and laid her eggs. She had forgotten about her tiny passenger until Hasina Binsaw slid off her back. Hasina crept down a corridor; at the last moment, she turned to wave goodbye. Yasura waved back, wondering whether the little ant had any hope of surviving in the teeming mound.

Yasura turned her attention back to the cocoons. During their incubation, her progeny would grow fat by consuming the caterpillar cocoons. Once her brood hatched, the caretakers of Antistan would raise the wasps as if they were members of the colony.

three

In a corridor deep within the burrowed structure of Antistan, Ashanti Lehana huddled with millions of her sisters just a few floors above the Queen. When the first bombs hit, all of the citizens had been in the Great Chamber listening to the President's daily oration. A million soldiers had raced to the surface, while nine million workers had retreated deeper into the mound, locking their bodies together to form a wall of flesh that would stymie enemy soldiers trying to reach the Queen.

Ashanti was wedged in so completely that she could not move any part of her body except her antennae. She watched wan sunlight filter through nearly invisible cracks in the mound; her eyes, perfectly suited for the environment, grabbed the meager light and amplified it to allow her to see clearly.

The attack had begun more than three hours ago, and Ashanti didn't know when it would end or what the outcome would be. Wars erupted regularly in Antistan, sometimes sparked by the aggression of neighboring colonies, sometimes by migratory tribes of army ants, sometimes by slave traders, and occasionally by internal tension. Ashanti was aware of the conflicts only to the extent that instinct compelled her to protect her Queen, but she had no interest in the political outcome of war. When the fighting ended, she would go back to her leaf-gathering duties with no concern about who had gained control of the presidency or who would now make decisions for the hive.

Ashanti had survived many wars, sitting exactly as she was now, her legs locked with those of her sisters, their bodies blocking the path to the Queen. If the enemy made it this far into the mound, Ashanti would give her own life without hesitation. She had no fear for her own safety. Her only concern was the survival of her Supreme Mother.

As soon as the war ended, Ashanti would race to the top to help clear the bodies from the battlefield, repair the damage to the mound, and return to her normal work duties. She spent every day marching into the foraging area and carrying back enormous leaves. She dropped them into a portal on the east side of the mound, where workers chopped them into pieces and carried them farther underground. There, smaller ants cut the leaves again and carried them deeper still; where the colony's tiniest ants laid them out and grew a mushroom-type fungus that provided a nutritious food supply for the entire mound. With a population of more than ten million ants, Antistan's daily consumption of vegetation equaled that of a full-grown wildebeest.

"What do you think is happening up there?" Victoria Abrey asked. "How do you think it's gonna turn out?" Her nervous, round face and worn mandibles betrayed her many years.

Ashanti shrugged. Though she was aware that the colony was under attack by a foreign force, she had no opinion about the conflict. Ashanti was a worker, not a thinker. She didn't waste her time speculating about what *might* exist or what *might* happen. She acted on instinct, and when she paused to contemplate anything at all, it was only to consider a specific task before her.

"I don't recognize the scent," Victoria said. Often the odor of the attacking army revealed its identity, but just as often the foreign scent wafting through the dark tunnels told the workers nothing.

Ashanti had a long, lean, athletic frame and thick mandibles shaped like a parrot's beak turned on its side. The serrated edges were perfect for grabbing and holding leaves. Her six long legs allowed her to stride down forest paths as if she were gliding. In the field, she could outrun most of her sisters, and she possessed uncommon strength for lifting, carrying, and pushing.

"If they get down here," Victoria said, "there's not much we can do, you know?"

Ashanti didn't respond.

"They'll rip us apart and carry our remains up to the surface one piece at a time," Victoria continued. "I hear they have mandibles that are half as long as their bodies, so they can grab you before you ever have a chance to fight back. And they can close down like this"—she slammed her jaws together in a loud clack—"and cut you in half without even trying."

Ashanti didn't ask who *they* were or how Victoria knew about their mandibles. Ashanti simply closed her mind to all distractions and focused on her duties. The workday was split into two overlapping shifts; the first started when the sun reached an angle of 5 degrees in the sky and continued until it hit 105 degrees. The second ran from 85 degrees to 175 degrees. The angle of the sun and the changing phases of the moon were the ants' only means of measuring time. They used the sun's golden glow to navigate back to the mound at the end of each day. Ashanti worked at a pace that left her breathless and weak when she finally surrendered for the day. The war was keeping her from gathering leaves, but Ashanti calculated that she could make up the lost time if she went to the Grotto foraging area rather than the Escalade. It was closer, so she could make more trips.

"Our mandibles just aren't made for fighting," Victoria lamented. "We could try to bite down, but it probably wouldn't even hurt them. The best we can do is just get in their way." Victoria tried to look around at all of her sisters, but she couldn't move her head in the tight space. "Don't you wonder who they are?" she asked. "Don't you wonder what colony they're from or why they decided to attack us?"

Ashanti didn't respond.

Victoria waved her antenna in the air. "Hey! That's fresh air!" She sniffed again. The rancid pheromones of the aliens were gone. "We've won!"

Four hours after the war had begun, clear colonial scent drifted through the underground channels. Ashanti uncorked her body and sprinted through the corridors with thousands of her sisters. They emerged, blinking in the late-day sun, and surveyed a battlefield littered with bodies.

Antistani soldiers stood on the surface staring at each other—some with their mandibles locked together—in dazed confusion. They released each other and wandered from place to place, looking at the devastation around them. Their big bodies bulged with muscles, but their combat-focused minds could not sort out the mystery of what had just happened. At one moment, there had been a war; the next moment the battle had ended and the enemy had retreated.

"All soldiers," a general bellowed, "secure the perimeter!" Relief washed over the faces of the baffled fighters. Securing the perimeter was a task they understood. They sprinted down the mound in every direction, racing across a clearing and into the surrounding foliage.

Ashanti Lehana set to work. She hoisted a dead soldier and stepped over thousands of corpses as she sprinted down the side of the mound to a dumpsite one coron toward the setting sun.

"Carry *bodies* out and *leaves* back!" Victoria shouted. Now that the war was over, Victoria didn't waste time with questions. She focused solely on her duties as a work leader.

The dead Antistan soldier in Ashanti's jaws was twice her size, but she carried him effortlessly, gripped just at the top of his metasoma. His head dangled at a precarious angle; it was clear that an enemy ant had dug his sharp pinchers into the soldier's neck. Ashanti kept a fast pace, but something nudged the edge of her consciousness. She pushed the thought away and concentrated on her work. She reached the dump and, without ceremony, dropped the soldier's body onto the growing pile. She turned back toward the mound, then stopped and ran east, having remembered Victoria's admonition to carry leaves back to the mound. She traveled about five minutes into the tall foliage and chose a mature leaf that was four times the length of her body. The triangular green leaf towered above her like a sail, and Ashanti expertly positioned it to catch the light wind and help propel her back toward the mound.

A flicker of a thought continued to claw at her concentration, but she shook her head to make it go away. Ashanti didn't deal in ideas or questions. She'd never wondered about the color of the sky, the great meaning of the universe, or even the efficacy of a particular policy. She had been born with the genes of a laborer; she saw herself simply as part of the machinery of the hive, and she did her job without thought or complaint. The unvarying nature of her duties gave her no more pause than a leaf might feel as the gatherer of sunlight for a tree.

Problem-solving was the province of special ants, so Ashanti had never *solved* anything. But now, something was burrowing deep into her consciousness, pushing her toward some unnamed question. She closed her eyes and groaned softly, not understanding the cause of this distraction. The leaf in her jaws slipped toward the ground. She tried to clutch it again, but her grip didn't catch until the leaf had tumbled too far. It toppled over, pulling her with it. She screamed out in alarm, and workers on the path scattered.

"Are you okay?" one of her sisters asked.

"I'm fine," Ashanti said. Embarrassment was another unfamiliar emotion, but she felt it all the same. "Just lost my grip." She did not say that it was her *concentration* that had slipped away from her. She didn't confess that her mind was so clouded with confusing thoughts that she couldn't complete a simple task that she'd performed effortlessly every day of her adult life. She shook her head, took a deep breath, and used all her strength to hoist the leaf back into the air.

She staggered down the path under the big sail and wondered why this ill-defined worry was tearing at her so persistently. She couldn't name the exact question that simmered inside her, but something about the appearance of the battlefield had struck her as odd. Ashanti had helped with post-war cleanup on many occasions, but this time when she had emerged into the sunlight, she'd sensed a subtle difference. Something didn't quite fit, but she could not put her antennae on it.

"It's . . .," she said aloud, but the question eluded her. The leaf in her mandibles slid forward again, hit the ground, and thudded sideways before Ashanti realized she'd lost it. The leaf crashed onto the path, blocking traffic.

"Be careful!" an older ant snapped as she stormed up and over the fallen leaf.

"I'm sorry," Ashanti said. Her face flushed. What was wrong with her? Why couldn't she concentrate? She raised the heavy leaf back into the air and cleared her mind. She marched toward the mound, focusing solely on the weight in her mandibles. Step after step she marched, down the path, and up the mound, weaving from side to side under the heavy leaf. Up and up she marched toward the battlefield.

"Ashanti!" Justine Tully said, rushing past to pick up another body. "What's wrong?"

"Nothing," Ashanti huffed. She marched up the steep slope.

"What's wrong with, Ashanti?" Laura Mejia asked.

"I don't know," Justine shrugged.

"That leaf"—Victoria boomed, pointing to the load in Ashanti's mandibles—"needs to go to the warehouse! Why did you bring it here to the battlefield?"

"Ashanti?" Justine said, brushing past her sister. "What are you doing?"

Suddenly, Ashanti sensed the problem. She dropped her leaf again and opened her mouth to speak.

"Not here!" Victoria rushed forward. "Take it to the warehouse!"

Ashanti's antennae danced quickly, sampling every pheromone wafting in the air of the battlefield. It was a soup of scents, but a key ingredient was missing.

"Where," Ashanti began slowly, twisting her head to the side as she formed the most difficult sentence of her life, "are . . . the . . . enemy . . . bodies?"

"What are you talking about? They're all over the pla . . .," Victoria started, but she lost her voice in the stark view before her. Her antennae vibrated rapidly, searching the air for molecules containing the scent of dead enemy soldiers, but she detected nothing. Victoria leaned over and touched a few corpses; they all bore the Antistani colonial scent.

During the war, the workers underground had smelled the powerful odor of a foreign army, but now on the battlefield, they could not smell a single enemy soldier.

"Where are the enemy bodies?" Ashanti asked again. She stood at rigid attention, her voice rising with each word. Now that the thought had emerged from her clouded mind, she spoke with clarity and confidence as if she'd been asking questions her entire life and was used to getting prompt answers.

By now, dozens of her sisters had stopped working. They, too, sampled the air with their antennae, and noted, with increasing shock, the peculiar, spectacular, unimaginable absence of enemy soldiers. They had all detected the enemy pheromone during the battle, but now all of the aliens had disappeared.

"Where are the enemy bodies?" Ashanti persisted. It was clear that she would continue to ask the question until someone provided an answer. When she opened her mouth to speak again, other workers joined her.

"WHERE ARE THE ENEMY BODIES?" they sang in a loud chorus.

"WHERE ARE THE ENEMY BODIES?" they chanted.

Dozens, then hundreds, then thousands of workers stood frozen, staring at the littered battlefield, screaming a question that few of them had the mental capacity to originate.

"WHERE ARE THE ENEMY BODIES?"

An ant half-buried in debris groaned.

"Someone is alive!" Ashanti raced toward him and dug feverishly at the pile. "Help me!" she screamed. Half a dozen workers dug with her, and soon they were able to pull the soldier out and set him gently on the soil. His head lolled to one side, and a wound gaped in his chest.

"Water," he gasped.

"Water!" Ashanti screamed.

A caretaker ran forward and produced a drop of fluid from her social stomach. She lowered her mouth to the soldier's face and gave him a drink.

"What happened here?" Ashanti said.

"Alpha Zee bombs," the ant groaned. "A wasp. Enemy everywhere."

"The Alpha Zee attacked us?" Victoria asked. "That's not possible."

"Why?" Ashanti asked. The question left her mouth without conscious thought, but once uttered it stole her breath. *Why?* Ashanti had never spoken the word. She'd never questioned her instructions, her duties, or any policy. But now, on the battlefield, in the aftermath of a bloody conflict, with a soldier dying at her feet but no enemy fighters in view, Ashanti's mind was swirling with *why*'s. "Why was it impossible for the Alpha Zee to have attacked?"

Victoria said, "Because they live more than eighty corons away. They can't mount an attack from that distance." She spoke as if she were an expert on military strategy.

"Are you sure it was the Alpha Zee?" Ashanti asked the soldier.

He nodded slowly. "Recognized their scent." The caretaker gave him another drink, and color washed over his ashen face. "They bombed us first—the formic acid on the rocks was definitely Alpha Zee."

"Then why are there no Alpha Zee bodies here?" Ashanti pointed at the battlefield.

"The Alpha Zee," the soldier said, gaining his voice, "didn't send in any ground forces. A wasp landed—"

"A wasp?" Victoria asked doubtfully. "Why would a wasp land in the middle of our hive? Our army would rip it to shreds."

The soldier nodded. "My platoon ran toward it, but when we got there, we encountered enemy fighters. We were caught by surprise because we didn't know where the invading force had come from." He coughed, and fluid seeped out of the hole in his chest. Ashanti didn't believe he would live much longer. "At one moment the wasp stood alone, and the next it was surrounded by enemy soldiers. It was almost as if—" the soldier hesitated.

"Almost as if what?" Ashanti prompted.

"No," the soldier said. "It's ridiculous." He shuddered and coughed again. His face creased with pain.

"Almost as if what?" Ashanti asked again. "Please."

The soldier sighed. His eyes fluttered. "It was almost as if," he said, "the wasp had transported hundreds of ants in its abdomen."

None of the workers laughed. On another day, at another time, in another mood, they might have had a good, long chuckle about the suggestion that ants could be ferried in the abdomen of a wasp. But the workers didn't laugh. They stood still, studying the injured ant with something that bordered on reverence. Ashanti didn't know what to make of the unfamiliar and uncomfortable feelings flooding her mind. She wondered if some secret knowledge was about to expire with this soldier. She wondered if the colony suffered a fractional decline each time a worker, a soldier, or a caretaker passed away. When the soldier at Ashanti's feet died, would the memory of this battle die with him? Would his death herald the loss of some critical information that the hive could never recover? Ashanti felt lightheaded under the weight of these strange and ponderous feelings. For the first time in her life, standing in the light caress of the sun, surrounded by thousands of her sisters, Ashanti Lehana felt the rough sinew of her own individuality. She was an ant—one unique ant, whose thoughts, feelings, and actions were distinct from those of her sisters and brothers.

"When did they retreat?" Victoria asked.

The fallen soldier didn't answer. He didn't move. He didn't open his eyes. He didn't breathe.

"They didn't retreat," a voice behind them said. The workers turned to face another soldier. One of his forelegs had been torn off; blood dripped from the wound. He grew pale as he talked. "The scent of attack started to fade and all of a sudden we were standing in the battlefield with our mandibles locked together with those of our brothers."

"It was an internal conflict?" Victoria was confused. How could that be? During the battle she had smelled alien fighters, and the other soldier had just told them that the Alpha Zee had dropped bombs.

"It wasn't a civil war," the soldier said. He grimaced and eased onto his side. "An outside enemy was here, but somehow they simply vanished, and we were left locked together as if we'd been fighting each other."

"I don't understand," Ashanti said.

The soldier shrugged, and that simple gesture seemed to exhaust him. Ashanti could see his life seeping away. "I've never seen this before, but I've heard of it," he said. "It's like a magic spell gets cast, and you're so blinded by it that you don't recognize the brothers and sisters you've been living with your entire life."

"That's ridiculous," Victoria said.

"Is it?" the soldier asked.

"Magic doesn't exist," Victoria said.

The soldier shrugged again and rested his head on the soft earth. His final question lingered in the air.

"We should get back to work," Ashanti said, her trembling voice unnerved the others. She picked up the leaf she'd dropped and headed across the battlefield to deliver it to the warehouse. The other workers picked up bodies and carried them away from the mound. Soon the hive was buzzing with activity once again, but Ashanti could not settle into the routine of labor. Her mind kept skipping from thought to thought, trying to make sense of the things that she had learned. Could there really be a magic spell that turned the colony against itself? Her newfound self-awareness prodded her urgently, as if the task of solving the riddle of this battle had been given to her by some greater power that would not let her retreat from this duty.

Why did the Alpha Zee tribe want Antistan to destroy itself?

four

Igniting civil wars in other colonies was not a typical Alpha Zee strategy, but its inter-colonial politics had transformed dramatically two years earlier, just after the birth of a deformed yet highly intelligent ant named Lucas Mallen.

For as long as anyone could remember, the army ants of Alpha Zee had been a migratory tribe, rolling across The Great Plain like a crimson plague, tearing apart insects, storming into rabbit warrens, capturing the eggs of ground-roosting birds and attacking rival ant hives. They continually conquered new territories, only to relinquish them a few weeks later when they had completely exhausted the hunting ground. Each afternoon as darkness approached, the Alpha Zee Senate ordered the colony to bivouac between the sheltering buttresses of raised tree roots or just inside the entrance of a hollowed log. Workers scrambled off the edges of the temporary shelter and dangled from their tarsal claws, extending their bodies. A second wave of ants climbed down the bodies of the first group and hung themselves from their brothers' and sisters' front legs. The workers continued this way, link upon link and layer upon layer until the entire colony was suspended in a tight cylinder of hard flesh with the Queen and her larvae tucked inside, protected against the wind, rain, and predators.

The colony typically stayed in each location for about three weeks, and when the hunters had exhausted all of the prey in the area, the Alpha Zee would embark upon a six- to seven-day migration to a new bivouac site. During the migration, the Queen's abdomen was almost as small as those of her many princesses, and she delivered no eggs. Eventually, the Alpha Zee Senate would conclude that the colony had migrated far enough, and the Senators would select a site that would serve as the Alpha Zee's bivouac home for the next three weeks. The Queen's abdomen would instantly begin to swell, and within an hour, she would start expelling a leathery cocoon every eight to ten seconds for a span of ten days. This was the rate necessary to maintain the tribe's population at roughly half a million citizens. After the arduous birthing cycle, the Queen fell into an exhausted sleep, and her abdomen began to slowly deflate. It would take another ten to twelve days for the juveniles to hatch, which was also about the time it would take for the tribe to consume all of the available food in the surrounding territory. As soon as the juveniles emerged, the Alpha Zee Colony would begin its next migration.

Lucas Mallen was born just after the rainy season, while the Alpha Zee tribe was bivouacked in the Kenobenoa Region of The Great Plain. The pheromone wafting up from his cocoon identified him as a soldier, and he spent the first week of his life nestled comfortably inside his egg, marveling at the sounds and scents all around him. He ravenously consumed the delicious white protein liquid until instinct told him that it was time to escape from his egg. He stabbed at the top of the cocoon, pressing toward the light, but he couldn't puncture the tough, spongy material.

Throughout the nursery, Mallen's brothers and sisters tore holes in their shells, and emerged to a shower of scent-praise from the caretakers, who groomed them and offered food. Mallen could smell the praise and the food, and he desperately longed for both. He kicked and clawed and pushed and scratched and screamed at his egg, but nothing worked. His shell seemed to be defective. There were no seams and no weak spots. The cocoon simply flexed when Mallen pushed against it, and then snapped back into its previous shape. He tried for hours, but eventually he collapsed, exhausted and discouraged.

Toward the end of the birthing day, the caretakers danced their antennae over the remaining cocoons. Each time they detected the scent of death they removed that egg and used it to feed the surviving members of the litter. Roughly twenty-five percent of the eggs were still-born and thus were converted into food, ensuring that no part of the Queen's labor went to waste.

But Lucas Mallen was still alive inside his cocoon. When the sun set at the end of the massive birthing day, his was the only cocoon remaining.

"We must leave him," the caretakers told the Alpha Zee Senate that evening. It pained them to abandon one of their charges, but they knew that the migration had to start immediately to find food for the newly born juveniles. It was too cold for Lucas Mallen to emerge during the night, so they knew that if he did finally escape, it wouldn't be until mid-morning the following day when the sun was high and the air was warm. The colony would be gone by then.

"Absolutely not!" General Edmund Gant barked. "Lucas Mallen is a *soldier*. We never leave one of our own behind."

Colonel Ainsley Walters was a hulking Alpha Zee fighter with long, serrated mandibles and an armored hide. Though his body had been built for combat, his mind was surprisingly agile and analytical. He listened to the debate about Mallen, wondering why no one had proposed a solution that seemed obvious to him. He stepped forward and said to President Alexander Kadira, "With your permission, sir, I'd like to visit the nursery to get an update on the situation." The Senate hadn't received a new report since nightfall. Though there was no chance that Lucas Mallen could have hatched in the cool evening temperature, he certainly could have died, which would render this debate moot.

"If something had changed, don't you think we would have heard from the caretakers?" President Kadira asked. He was flanked, as usual, by his three advisors—the Secretaries of State, Defense and Bivouac Security. Colonel Walters thought of them as a single, multi-headed creature, because they always spoke together, as if they shared one brain and stretched each thought between them. They parroted the President, but added a contemptuous sneer to everything that he said.

"Yeah," the Secretary of State said, "we would have—"

"—heard from the caretakers," the Secretary of Defense continued.

"Or can't you figure that out?" the Secretary of Bivouac Security finished.

"You're probably right," Colonel Walters conceded. "However, there are no senior officers in the nursery right now. Every decision-maker is here in the Senate. It's entirely possible that Lucas Mallen's situation has changed, but no one has had the initiative or the authority to alert us."

President Kadira quietly conferred with his Secretaries. "Okay, Colonel Walters," he said finally. "Go get us a status report."

Colonel Walters climbed up the wide bivouac cylinder to the nursery, which was located near the top to keep the eggs and the juveniles warm. A phalanx of soldiers stood guard around the lone remaining cocoon.

"He's one of *ours*, sir!" the soldiers said, saluting.

Colonel Walters wanted to tell them that *every* citizen was one of theirs, not just the soldiers, but he simply saluted back. He asked the caretakers how the other juveniles were doing. The colony's youngest citizens were huddled together, sleeping through their first cool night outside of their eggs.

"They're fine at the moment, sir," one of the caretakers said, "but if we don't start the migration first thing in the morning, we could lose a third of them."

"Is Mallen still alive?" Colonel Walters asked.

"Yes, sir. His scent is weak, but he's alive."

Colonel Walters returned to the Alpha Zee Senate; the members grew quiet when he entered. "We should start the migration at daybreak," Colonel Walters said.

"Mallen is dead?" President Kadira asked.

"No, sir. He's still alive."

"You're proposing that we leave a *soldier* behind?" General Gant thundered, incredulously.

The Secretaries asked, "*You* would—"

"—*abandon*—"

"—one of your *own*?"

"I would never suggest that," Colonel Walters said patiently. "Someone will simply have to carry him."

A murmur rustled through the Senate.

President Kadira shook his head. "We can't carry him. Every ant must run under his own power. The migration is an important test for the juveniles. Only the fittest will survive, and the weak will be eliminated. Carrying a citizen is forbidden. It would allow a weaker ant to survive, and that would compromise the overall strength of the tribe."

"Yeah," the Secretary of State said. "Are you—"

"—trying to—" The Secretary of Defense continued.

"—weaken us?" The Secretary of Bivouac Security finished.

"I suggest that we carry him tomorrow to the next bivouac site," Colonel Walters said. "That will solve our immediate dilemma. We won't have to violate the military oath by leaving him behind, and we won't have to watch a third of our litter perish waiting for him to emerge from his shell. The caretakers have confirmed that the food inside Mallen's cocoon is gone, so tomorrow he will either break free or starve to death. If we carry him for one day, we can let nature take its course."

"No ant gets carried!" President Kadira said, clacking his mandibles forcefully, ending the discussion on that point.

"And no *soldier* gets left behind!" General Gant said, clacking his mandibles even harder, ending the discussion on *that* point.

Colonel Walters sighed. He was often frustrated by the fact that the Alpha Zee's leaders, who were generally wise and experienced, could get locked into simple, ideological positions and completely lose their ability to consider alternate solutions.

"Then may I make one other suggestion?" Colonel Walters asked.

"What is it?' President Kadira asked impatiently.

"Why don't we open Mallen's shell for him?"

"Absolutely not!" the President cried.

The Secretaries screamed, "Ab-so—,"

"—*lutely*—,"

"—not!"

"There is no rite of passage more sacred than escaping from one's own shell!" President Kadira said. "Every ant must do it for himself. If Mallen can't get out of his shell, then he wasn't meant to be here."

"He's a soldier!" General Gant said, glaring at Colonel Walters. "Think of the humiliation he'll feel if he has to be rescued from his own egg."

The Secretaries asked, "Are you—,"

"—trying to—"

"—humiliate him?"

"I'm less worried about his ego than I am about the fate of the colony," Colonel Walters replied.

"You're out of line, soldier!" President Kadira barked.

Colonel Walters nodded, and backed away, blending into a group of Senators.

The entire colony slept fitfully through the night, anxious about what would happen to Lucas Mallen in the morning. Once the sun crested the horizon, the temperature of his egg would climb steadily, and when the sun reached an angle of 23 degrees in the sky, it would be warm enough for him to escape. But would he?

At first light, the entire colony released itself from the tight cylinder and crowded around Lucas Mallen's egg. The juveniles moaned with hunger pangs. The soldiers paced anxiously. Everyone could sense that it was time to leave, but they couldn't depart until Mallen either escaped or died.

As soon as Lucas Mallen woke up, he started pounding on his shell. He was starving and desperate, but nothing he tried worked. He could smell the ants all around him. He begged for their help. But they merely watched as the skin of his cocoon bulged and rippled.

Finally, crying, he collapsed, surrendering to the realization that he would die in his tiny chamber.

Colonel Walters was among the soldiers standing closest to the cocoon. "This is ridiculous," he muttered under his breath. With an effortless swipe of his mandibles, he tore a hole in the top of the egg.

General Edmund Gant glared at Colonel Walters. "What do you think you're doing?"

Colonel Walters ignored his superior and said, "Come on out, Lucas Mallen! You're holding up the whole parade."

Warm sunlight spilled into the egg, and Mallen emerged slowly, exhausted, gasping for breath. One of the caretakers stepped forward to give him some food from her social stomach, but she stopped suddenly, staring in amazement. Everyone in the nursery gasped, and for several long moments, no one spoke or emitted a scent.

Lucas Mallen, blinking in the light, was unaware that he was grotesquely deformed. The shape of his head was normal, as were his antenna and eyes. But he was missing the most dominant and most important feature that any ant possessed.

Lucas Mallen had no mandibles.

He had a small moist mouth, surrounded by tiny hairs, but he didn't even have small nubs on the side of his face that would have indicated the beginnings of mandibles. The citizens of Alpha Zee were known for their sharp, arching mandibles that could cut through the thick carapace of any enemy. Every soldier, every forager, every caretaker, and even the Queen was armed with a set of deadly pinchers. Lucas Mallen was the first ant they'd ever seen who didn't have a set.

"Kill him," General Gant said, turning away, disgusted.

"But he's one of *our own*," Colonel Walters reminded him.

"He's not a soldier," General Gant said. Several soldiers moved forward, clacking their mandibles, but Colonel Walters stepped in front of them, protecting the newborn citizen. The soldiers stopped and stared up at the big colonel, unsure what to do.

Colonel Walters turned to one of the elder caretakers and asked, "What do you normally do with ants who are deformed?"

The caretaker looked uncomfortable. "The truth? We leave them behind."

Colonel Walters refused to accept that answer, "We should let the Queen decide his fate."

"There's nothing to decide!" General Gant barked. "A soldier without mandibles is like a lion without teeth. He's a liability. Kill him and let's start the migration."

Colonel Walters stood his ground.

"I'm giving you a direct order!" General Gant said.

Colonel Walters said, "You're giving me an *unjust* order."

"Justice? You're a soldier. You kill every day of your life. Who are you to talk about justice?"

"We don't kill innocent civilians. Tell your soldiers to stand down."

"Now you're giving *me* orders?" General Gant asked incredulously.

Colonel Walters ignored the question. He turned to one of the caretakers and asked her to give Mallen some food. She nodded obediently and offered Mallen trophallaxis. The juvenile gobbled it down greedily. Then Colonel Walters picked up the small ant in his mandibles and eased through the tense throng of soldiers. He carried Mallen to the Queen's guarded area.

President Kadira was standing with his antennae intertwined with the Queen's; they were having a private scent conversation. He looked up as Colonel Walters entered with Lucas Mallen held aloft.

"What do we have here?" President Kadira asked.

Colonel Walters didn't look at the President. His eyes were locked on the Queen. "I have your newest citizen, your Majesty."

I can see that, the Queen said with a gentle scent. She never used her voice; she spoke only through elegantly crafted pheromones.

"He has no mandibles!" General Gant yelled from the entrance to the Queen's chamber.

SO PUT HIM TO DEATH, President Kadira said, showing off with his own ability to speak through scents. But the odors he produced were crude and simplistic. He lacked the Queen's subtlety and grace, so it sounded as if he were shouting.

That seems a bit harsh, the Queen said. The warmth of her pheromones washed over Lucas Mallen, and he felt as if nourishment was seeping through his pores.

HE CAN'T KILL, SO WHAT USE IS HE? President Kadira asked.

"Yeah," the Secretaries repeated,

"—what good—"

"—is he?"

Is that the only criteria by which to judge the usefulness of our fellow citizens? the Queen asked.

WE'RE ARMY ANTS, YOUR EMINENCE, President Kadira said. *KILLING IS THE BASIC BUILDING BLOCK OF OUR SURVIVAL.*

I've never killed anyone, the Queen said.

THAT'S DIFFERENT.

Is it?

OF COURSE. YOU HAVE MUCH MORE IMPORTANT DUTIES TO PERFORM.

Perhaps Lucas Mallen has more important duties as well.

WHAT CAN HE POSSIBLY DO?

"He couldn't even escape from his shell!" General Gant shouted.

HOW DID HE GET OUT? President Kadira asked.

"Colonel Walters disobeyed a direct order and sliced open the shell," General Gant reported.

IS THAT TRUE, COLONEL? President Kadira asked.

"Yes, it is," Colonel Walters said. "I felt that continuing to wait for him put the colony at too much risk."

SO WHY HAVE YOU BROUGHT THIS USELESS LITTLE ANT HERE?

"Justice demands that we give Queen Wenonah the opportunity to determine his fate."

"Justice?" President Kadira laughed, using his voice.

Colonel Walters didn't laugh. Neither did the Queen. From the start of her reign, Queen Wenonah had infused each new cocoon with a simple pheromone code that compelled her progeny to deal *justly* with their fellow tribe members. The pheromone ensured that each citizen had the right to a fair ration of food; the right to be assigned a specific task within the caste structure of the hive, and the right to a hearing with the Queen before being executed for the commission of a crime. However, the pheromone was imprinted only on the Queen's direct descendents, which now comprised about 35 percent of the tribe. The other 65 percent were her siblings, who had left the Yumana hive with her three years ago when she departed to form the Alpha Zee Colony.

"The Queen's *justice code*—"

"—doesn't apply—"

"—in this situation," the Secretaries said.

"That's right," the President said. "Mallen doesn't have any mandibles, so there's no job that he can perform, *and* he's not going to be executed because of a crime."

"He'll be executed—" The Secretaries explained,

"—because he never should have—"

"—been born in the first place."

"He's a threat to tribal security," the President said.

Colonel Walters ignored the President and the Secretaries. He stepped close to Queen Wenonah, who smiled up at him. Walters was her younger brother, and since birth, he had been a free-thinking ant, who asked questions, and refused to blindly follow orders. The hive certainly couldn't function with *many* ants like Colonel Walters, but Queen Wenonah believed that Alpha Zee benefited from his periodic challenges. He was intelligent, reasonable, and compassionate, which were remarkable characteristics for an ant born with the genes of a soldier.

She wasn't sure what she should do about Lucas Mallen. Although Queen Wenonah was the most powerful *individual* in Alpha Zee, the Senate was the tribe's ultimate authority. The Senate chose the site of the bivouacs, determined the scope, direction, and duration of all hunting expeditions, and mandated the distribution of food. Queen Wenonah obeyed the Senate's scent decrees as automatically as the rest of the citizens. She had three primary responsibilities—to set the overall scent of the tribe, to create a unique scent tag for each caste and each individual, and to deliver workers, warriors and caretakers according to the percentages mandated by the Senate.

Queen Wenonah carefully studied the tiny ant cradled in Colonel Walters' mandibles. The Queen knew that no matter what she decided, Lucas Mallen's future was bleak. With no mandibles and no way to contribute to the hive, he would likely fall into fatal depression. Every ant took great pride in making a contribution to the hive. That was the reason that Queen Wenonah had included a responsibility decree and the right to work as part of the justice code. For an ant, *not* working was worse than a death sentence.

She exhaled slowly. Mallen couldn't perform as a soldier, forager, or caretaker, and those were the three primary castes. General Gant was right. If nature had taken its course, Lucas Mallen never would have escaped from his shell, and the Queen wouldn't be faced with this dilemma.

"Every ant has a purpose," Colonel Walters said, quietly. "You have the power to decide *his*, Majesty."

But what can he do? she asked in a gentle pheromone whisper.

The colonel shrugged. "Something that doesn't require mandibles."

The Queen shook her head wearily, because she didn't know of any jobs in Alpha Zee that didn't require mandibles, but suddenly, she smiled and then laughed. The powerful scent of her laughter cascaded over all of the citizens, causing all of them to laugh with her. With a flick of her antennae, the Queen stripped away Lucas Mallen's soldier scent tag and covered him with pheromones that identified him as an "alarm lookout." The formal position *Alarm Lookout* had never existed in Alpha Zee, so this chemical concoction was a brilliant new creation. Typically, lookouts were ad hoc positions assigned each day by the military leaders.

Colonel Walters smiled warmly at his Queen. "A wonderful choice, Majesty." He turned back to the assembled throng, and said, "Queen Wenonah has given us our first full-time alarm lookout!"

No one quite knew what that meant, but it didn't matter. Lucas Mallen's new scent tag silenced any further discussion about his fate. A lookout didn't need mandibles. Lucas Mallen would spend his days sitting high above the colony, watching for the approach of enemies.

Immediately, the Senate ordered the colony to depart for the migration. The entire tribe set off toward the west in a three-foot wide rippling river of maroon flesh.

General Gant moved up beside Colonel Walters and said, "You're going to get demoted tonight! I am the ranking officer in this military, and, when I give you a direct order, I expect—"

"General," Colonel Walters interrupted, "demote me if you must, but I will object whenever I believe that your orders are unjust."

"Your insubordination is astounding!" General Gant growled. "This time you will pay for your disrespect."

But Colonel Walters did not pay. When the Senate met that evening, President Kadira introduced a motion to strip Colonel Walters of his rank, but the Senate rebelled.

"He deserves a *promotion*," one senator cried.

"For repeatedly disobeying direct orders?" President Kadira asked incredulously.

"We should make him a general!" someone else yelled, drawing applause from the assembled leaders.

President Kadira waved his front legs, trying to regain control of the group. Clearly the Senate didn't understand how the military was supposed to function. They reacted with their emotions rather than their minds. The President said, "What message will we be sending to the rest of the troops if the colonel is promoted immediately after this display of disobedience?"

"Besides we've never had more than one general at a time," General Edmund Gant argued. "And this is *my* time!"

But the Senators insisted that Colonel Walters deserved the promotion because his initiative had saved Lucas Mallen's life, allowed the hive to begin its migration before the juveniles started dying, and led to the creation of the colony's first dedicated alarm lookout.

"He's an Alpha Zee hero!" the Senators declared as they voted to make General Ainsley Walters one of the two most powerful ants in the Alpha Zee Military.

five

Each morning a third of the Alpha Zee foragers and soldiers raced off toward the frayed cuff of sunlight on the horizon, while everyone else stayed behind to protect the Queen and the pupae. As zebras whinnied and wildebeests shook their thick heads, the ants of Alpha Zee chased down grasshoppers, spiders, beetles, caterpillars and alien ants and carried them back to the campsite to feed the tribe.

Lucas Mallen watched the action from his elevated perch. He envied his siblings for their speed, their power, and their freedom to run through the tall grass, but, as much as he wished that he could join them, he took his job as a lookout seriously. He scanned the horizon with professional diligence. If any threat approached the hive, Mallen was determined to be the first to spot it and raise the alarm.

But while he watched for predators and aliens, he also marveled at the careful interplay between the various castes of the Alpha Zee tribe. He knew that the Queen was the hive's most important citizen, but he couldn't decide which caste was the second in importance. At first, he thought that the foragers were most vital, because they brought home the food that fed everyone. But then Mallen realized that without the caretakers, the foragers would never have survived their juvenile stage, so perhaps it was the caretakers who were most important since they nurtured each new generation into adulthood. But, of course, the caretakers were ill-equipped to defend against an attacking army. Without the soldiers, any enemy could walk into the bivouac site and kill the Queen, and without the Queen, the colony would die. So perhaps the soldiers were the most important of all. Without them, none of the citizens could feel secure. After a week of debating the issue with himself Mallen finally concluded that it was impossible to place one caste above the others, because each ant contributed his or her best effort for the greater good of the hive, and each caste depended on the others.

This realization buoyed Mallen's spirits, because his internal debate about the castes was really an examination of his role in the tribe. The conclusion that everyone contributed something important put him at ease, and he began to relish the sheer pleasure of watching the world around him. He loved the way honeybees lumbered through the air with pollen-covered legs, landing awkwardly on flowers, before revving up their tiny wings and buzzing off again in zigzagging flight.

He laughed at the oxpecker birds, perched on the backs of buffaloes. Sometimes as many as a dozen squawked in loud arguments as they fought for position aboard a particular beast. Once when the colony was bivouacked near a river, Mallen watched an Egyptian plover bird walk casually into the open jaws of a crocodile that was basking on the bank. The crocodile didn't react as the plover hopped all around its mouth, pecking at scraps of food trapped between the crocodile's enormous teeth. When the bird was full, it calmly stepped out and flew away. Then the crocodile closed its jaws and slid quietly back into the water. Mallen shook his head. What an incredible world!

Once, just after the tribe had settled in a new location, Mallen watched as the Queen slowly pumped her abdomen full of eggs. Every few minutes, her stomach would ripple and its circumference would increase, until finally, long white cylinders started popping out of the narrow opening at the back of her gaster. Each was ferried away by the caretakers. The Queen seemed exhausted by the effort, but she kept pushing, knowing that she had to keep pace with the colony's high mortality rate.

From his high perch, Lucas Mallen watched the delicate interaction between the plants, the animals, and the weather. He could see farther than any other ant in the colony. Yes, the winged males could fly, but they couldn't stay aloft for hours at a time, and they had to constantly shift their attention. Mallen watched the foragers depart and return, the Queen and her coterie of caretakers, the swarms of insects trying to escape from the hunters, the herds of mammals, and the swaying groves of trees.

He started to notice patterns in the way that the wind pushed the clouds into different shapes—sometimes thin and flat, sometimes fluffy and white, other times towering and grey. If the wind was in his face and dark clouds bubbled on the horizon, Mallen warned his brothers and sisters that rain was coming. At first, the Senate had been reluctant to recall the foragers based on Mallen's predictions, but after thousands of foragers and soldiers were killed in a storm that Mallen had forecast, the Senate began to pay more attention to his warnings.

Mallen learned that the rapid movement of animals such as antelopes usually revealed the presence of lions or cheetahs, whose kills could provide protein for the Alpha Zee if the felled animal was close enough. If Mallen saw Savannah sparrows swooping toward the ground in the distance, he knew that they must be feeding on grasshoppers, one of the Alpha Zee's favorite meals. Mallen shared this information with the President, who used it to set the direction of the colony's next migration.

When he saw honeydew radiating off distant plants like droplets of molten sunlight, he told the Senate that herds of aphids must be in the area. The Alpha Zee loved the taste of aphids and the gooey honeydew that they produced, so the following morning, foragers raced out in the direction that Mallen had indicated and came home with scores of aphids.

If Mallen saw a herd of elephants, he knew that the pachyderms would be trailed by thousands of flying dung beetles. The beetles would land on piles of manure, roll the dung into balls and bury themselves with their three- or four-day food supply. Hunting dung beetles was as close to farming as the migratory Alpha Zee tribe ever got. The Senate ordered the foragers to travel in the elephants' wake, where they dug up beetles as if they were harvesting tubers. If the Queen hadn't been required to stay in one spot for several weeks each month to deliver her eggs, the Alpha Zee might have adopted trailing elephants as a permanent strategy.

In just a few months, Lucas Mallen established himself as much more than an alarm lookout. As he observed life on The Great Plain, he made inferences that seemed like magic to his peers. In recognition of his special contribution, the Queen summoned him to the birthing area, which was encircled by a platoon of soldiers. The fighters frisked Mallen suspiciously before allowing him to enter. Because he sat in one spot every day and got no exercise, Mallen had grown quite large. He waddled toward the Queen and felt her powerful but light pheromones lapping against his chitinous skin in gentle waves. He noted that her head and thorax were about the same size as those of a typical reproductive female, but her abdomen was an enormous, distended bulb that pulsed with the future lifeblood of the colony.

Greetings, she said with a pheromone that sent a shiver of pleasure down Lucas Mallen's antennae. *When you were born, I knew that you were special.* Mallen couldn't respond to his Supreme Mother. He was rendered mute by her powerful chemical emissions. His eyes fluttered madly and he swayed, barely conscious in front of her. *I never would have guessed that giving you the tag of a lookout would have ignited your wonderful intellect in the way that it has. I am so proud of you. You possess wisdom that is more powerful than even the strongest set of mandibles. Your insights have made us a better tribe. Thank you for your contribution."*

Mallen slumped to the ground, overwhelmed by this chemical praise. Several caretakers picked him up and carried him back to the perimeter of the bivouac site, where soldiers ran their antennae over him, sniffing again, but now with respect rather than suspicion. The pheromone radiating from his body declared that he was one of the leaders of the Alpha Zee Colony.

Several weeks later, Lucas Mallen spotted a splash of color on the bland turf of the prairie. In the distance, three enormous baobab trees with half-moon canopies sheltered an oasis of grass, sunflowers, and prickly weeds, all waving gently in the breeze. Mallen inferred the presence of a pond not visible from his vantage point; it was the only explanation for the lush dark green plants. At this time of year, the Alpha Zee could make great use of a pond. The colony normally harvested all of its water from the dew standing on grass and leaves early in the morning, but that produced only enough water for drinking, not bathing.

The Senate dispatched a group of scouts in the direction of the oasis, and when they returned, it was obvious that they had bathed in the pond. Weeks of accumulated grime had been washed away from their bodies, their carapaces gleamed, and their faces were flushed with healthy color.

"The pond is clean and clear," one of the scouts said. "There are no predators in the area—and there's a driver ant hive just one coron from the water."

"How big is the mound?" President Kadira asked. Driver ant larvae were delicious, and the prospect of sating the Alpha Zee's hunger and thirst at the same time made the President's antennae twitch with excitement.

"Based on the dimensions of the physical structure and the number of foragers we observed in the field, we estimate the population at about two million citizens."

President Kadira nodded slowly, calculating the size of the driver ant military. It would be much larger than the Alpha Zee fighting force, but that was okay, because the Alpha Zee was a tribe of specialized warriors. They were well-trained, well-armed and easily capable of defeating armies ten times larger than themselves. The driver-ant military would present little challenge.

President Kadira conferred with the Senate for a few minutes and emerged to tell the citizens, "We'll attack at dawn."

At first light, the raiding party stormed away from the bivouac site in what looked like a regular full-colony migration. Most of the soldiers were out front, followed by the foragers, and Queen Wenonah, her caretakers, and a protective guard. After the battle, the Alpha Zee would move into the driver-ant hive and use it as a new bivouac site.

The fight didn't last long. Alpha Zee soldiers effortlessly sliced through the driver ant military and then pushed past the defenseless workers until they reached the rival Queen. She was spread-eagled and torn apart with cold indifference.

Queen Wenonah arrived just after the mound was secured and was quickly escorted into a deep, safe chamber. The citizens of Alpha Zee immediately began gorging themselves on the driver ant larvae, seeds, dried fruits, berries, vegetables, nectar, and sap in the driver-ants' warehouses. The Alpha Zee were primarily carnivorous, but their digestive systems were adaptive enough to tolerate fruits and vegetables if acquiring the food didn't require great effort.

As he chewed on a juicy berry, Lucas Mallen wandered through the corridors of the mound, marveling at the impressive structure. Mallen had been inside three other ant hives, following previous Alpha Zee conquests, but this was, by far, the most elaborate. The dark earthen structure had a hard crust to protect it from wind and rain, yet, inside, the soil was comfortably moist even in the middle of this long, hot, dry season. Its air channeling system kept even the deepest chambers at a moderate temperature. A drainage system channeled rainwater into an underground reservoir while the excess sluiced harmlessly over the sides of the mound. Enormous warehouses held a wide array of non-perishable food, an infirmary was filled with medicinal plants, and a carefully managed waste removal system kept the hive clean.

Lucas Mallen couldn't help musing about the comfortable life the Alpha Zee would enjoy if the tribe lived permanently in this mound rather than constantly relocating to new bivouac sites. Queen Wenonah wouldn't have to endure the arduous mass birthing cycle. Instead, she could relax in her royal chamber and dispense eggs at a more leisurely pace.

Mallen sighed, knowing that this was an unrealistic fantasy. The Alpha Zee survived on a diet of meat and honey-dew—the sources of which rarely stood still, and which they quickly exhausted—so the tribe had to move continually to locate new prey. But, for now, they would stay in this mound for weeks or months—however long it took to consume all of the food.

The driver ant caretakers, workers, and foragers still roamed freely in the mound. They hadn't been killed, because they presented no threat to the Alpha Zee, and they were not suitable for eating. Despite the death of their Queen and the occupation by a foreign tribe, the driver ants continued to maintain the mound, and collect food. Instinct compelled them to work, and Lucas Mallen watched their activity curiously. He had noted the continued productivity of ants in other hives that the Alpha Zee had commandeered, but this time, Mallen had an insight that had eluded him in the past. He stood up, smiling, and waddled down to the Senate chambers.

Mallen was breathing heavily when he finally reached the governmental chamber. He listened carefully as the Senators calculated the exact amount of time that the Alpha Zee would stay in the mound. Most of the Senators seemed to believe that there might be enough food to support the Alpha Zee for three full moons.

Lucas Mallen interrupted: "We should consider living here permanently."

"Don't be ridiculous," President Kadira said. "This may be the most food we've ever seen stored up, but it will run out eventually."

"But, sir," Mallen continued, "their foragers are still collecting food."

"Yes, but not enough to sustain us. Their Queen is dead, so they don't have her dominant pheromones to focus their attention, and they no longer have a Senate to guide them with scent decrees, so their foraging patterns are haphazard and not very efficient. More of them get lost in the field every day, so the volume of their collections is decreasing. Even though they look healthy and alive, they're dying. Their movements have no more meaning than the twitching limbs of a headless body."

"What if we attached a new head?" Mallen asked.

"What do you mean?" President Kadira frowned.

"Couldn't we shift their scent loyalty to Queen Wenonah?"

"Yes, we could," the President said disdainfully, "but we don't enslave foreign workers."

"We—"

"—just—"

"—watch them die!" the Secretaries added.

"They wouldn't be slaves," Mallen said. "They'd be fellow citizens."

"Citizens? Impossible!" President Kadira boomed. "They're not *army* ants!"

"No, but they *are* experts at building and maintaining a mound," Mallen said. "And they're good at foraging for food."

"But they could never gather enough food to feed us," the President argued. "Even if they can supplement our diet, we'll still have to go hunting, and we'll still eventually deplete all the prey within a half-day's march of here."

"And shifting their allegiance to Queen Wenonah—"

"—would blur the line between us and them—"

"—so how would we know who was a legitimate citizen and who was a foreigner?" the Secretaries challenged.

"Why would we care?" Mallen responded. "In our tribe every ant is born into a particular caste and that division of labor is beneficial to all of us, because it allows each of us to focus on our natural strengths. The driver ants could become another caste in our society. They constructed this hive, so they know how to run it. They could build the tunnels, remove waste, collect food and water, and perform all of the other critical duties of the mound. In exchange, they get to live with us in safety, because our military will protect them."

"But they're not *army* ants!" the President bellowed. "Our caste system works, because we're all part of the same species and the same family. You're talking about two different species cooperating in a way that is completely unnatural. The only way that could possibly work is if we turned them into slaves, and that's not going to happen, because we're not slave-makers!"

Lucas Mallen paused for a moment, trying to organize the thoughts swirling in his head. He knew that the President was correct in one manner of thinking. The Alpha Zee didn't have the temperament required to enslave another tribe. But Mallen had observed partnerships on The Great Plain that made him realize that creatures of different species *could* live together peacefully, without enslavement.

So Mallen spoke about the butterflies and bees who collected delicious nectar from flowers, while carrying pollen from bloom to bloom to help the flowers reproduce. He told them about the oxpecker birds who rode on backs of buffaloes, eating ticks and other parasites. The birds got an easy meal, while the buffaloes received much-needed grooming. He told them about the Egyptian plover birds that waded into the steamy mouths of crocodiles. The birds got nutritious meals, while the reptiles got their teeth cleaned. He told them about troops of monkeys swinging through the trees, plucking and eating ripe fruits. The monkeys received a sweet meal, and some of the seeds they dropped to the ground eventually sprouted into new trees.

"These are all unconscious partnerships," Mallen explained. "These creatures aren't aware that they're exchanging anything. But I believe that we could consciously create an alliance with the citizens of this driver ant mound that would allow both tribes to live here permanently."

The President and the Secretaries were opposed to the idea, but many of the Senators seemed intrigued. The Senate asked Mallen and all the other non-politicians to leave the chamber so that they could discuss the proposal. Several hours later the Senate emerged and announced that the Alpha Zee would experiment with Mallen's suggestion during the current bivouac. The driver ants and their pupae would remain in the hive, but only as second-class citizens. Queen Wenonah would create a special scent tag which would give them safe passage among the Alpha Zee, but it would distinguish them from regular citizens. Their scent would compel them to move to the back of any food line, occupy the hottest chambers in the summer and the coldest in the winter, and surrender the contents of their social stomachs to any full-blooded Alpha Zee citizen who demanded it. The Senate also ordered that all of the *reproductive* driver ants be executed at birth.

"Why?" Lucas Mallen asked.

"We don't want them to multiply," President Kadira said.

"But we *need* them to reproduce," Mallen said. "It will take many generations of driver ants to maintain this hive in the years to come."

"No," a Senator said, "We just need them to train our workers, and then we'll take over."

Mallen shook his head. "The mandibles of our citizens are designed for hunting and fighting—not digging. We need the driver ants."

"But if they *multiply*, they'll eventually outnumber us by too great a margin," President Kadira warned.

"And how could you dare suggest—"

"—that we have more than one—"

"—queen!" the Secretaries screeched.

Lucas Mallen said, "Queen Wenonah would be the dominant mother. She'll set the scent for everybody, including a lesser scent for the princesses who will become queens. When the reproductive season starts, we'll require one of the pregnant princesses to stay here to become a secondary queen. She'll continue to produce caretakers, workers, princes and princesses—but no soldiers."

This plan seemed too complicated to most of the citizens to understand, but the Senate agreed to try it since the tribe was going to be bivouacked in the hive for three moons anyway.

"One other thing," Mallen said. "Today I saw a herd of aphids just five corons west of here."

The Senate broke into rapturous applause. Aphids were among the Alpha Zee's favorite meals. The insects' bodies were full of honeydew so biting through the meaty outer layer led to a sweet, gooey center.

"We should visit the aphids tomorrow morning," Mallen continued.

A murmur swept through the Senate. *Visit?* The colony had never *visited* prey.

In the morning, the hunters set out at a leisurely walking pace, which was as fast as Lucas Mallen could travel. When they got close to the herd of aphids, Mallen ordered the hunters to encircle the creatures.

"But don't touch them," he whispered.

Mallen and several members of the Senate entered the clearing and walked toward the herd. The panicked aphids tried to escape, but they quickly realized that they were trapped. They looked at the enormous force of army ants surrounding them and cried in despair.

"Don't worry," Lucas Mallen said, smiling, "we're not here to eat you."

The aphids stopped crying at once. They spoke the same scent language as the ants, yet this was the first time the murderous hunters had ever spoken to them. A few aphids had escaped from swarming hordes in the past, and they had described the attackers as a wave of molten lava—never hesitating, never negotiating, and *always* killing everything in its path. But now the ants had initiated a conversation.

"What do you want?" asked an elder aphid, who had gray eyes and a rounded back. He studied Mallen carefully. He had never before seen an army ant without mandibles.

"We want you to come live with us," Mallen said.

The elder looked around. Hundreds of thousands of ants stood in the tall grass. 'Why would we do that?"

"Because we can protect you from other predators."

The elder thought about that answer for a moment. "Why would *you* do that?"

"Because you have honeydew."

Aphids were herbivores that expelled droplets of honeydew as waste. It dripped onto plants and onto the prairie floor and mixed with the droppings of other insects. The elder knew that bees, butterflies, and honeypot ants collected honeydew—but army ants? As far as he knew, army ants ate only flesh. He'd seen enough of his friends and family torn apart to be certain of that brutal fact.

"There's honeydew all over," the elder said, pointing at the surrounding foliage. "We've been grazing here for three days, and we've dropped a lot of it. Take what you want."

"We want more than that," Mallen said.

The elder shook his head. "That's all there is."

"No," Mallen said. "There's plenty more inside of you."

The aphids moaned and drew closer together.

"Do you mean to rip us open and drink from our torn bodies?" the elder asked. He was a pacifist by nature, but his eyes gleamed with rage.

"No," Mallen said, smiling. "We don't want to hurt you. Quite the opposite. We want you to come live with us and graze under our protection in a delicious, garden of grass and flowers."

The elder aphid squinted at him. "What's the catch?"

"There is no catch," Mallen said. "We need honeydew, and you need a safe place to live. It's a partnership."

The elder nodded. It was a good plan, but it had a flaw that could prove fatal for his family. "There are so few of us, and so many of you. We can never produce enough honeydew to feed all of you." He knew that when the ants grew hungry enough they would simply eat the flock of aphids.

Mallen smiled again. "With our protection, you'll multiply quickly."

The elder looked around again at the swarm of Alpha Zee soldiers. He had to concede that if Mallen was telling the truth about the Alpha Zee's intentions, then captivity *could* be a very good life. His family had always lived in constant fear of predators; it would be a welcome relief to gain the protection of such a powerful army.

So the aphids marched back to the mound and grazed in a protected paddock. Caretakers tended the herd, collecting droplets of honeydew whenever the aphids released them.

six

The Alpha Zee settled into the mound and scouted the lush territory around the pond, which the Senate officially named "The Grove." The oasis of vegetation covered more than 10,000 square corons and was home to twelve other ant mounds—seven driver ant hives, four honeypot tribes, and one leafcutter mound. Every time the Alpha Zee ran low on protein, the hunters and soldiers charged into one of the nearby hives, killed the rival army and claimed a bounty of larvae. The Alpha Zee also consumed a portion of its continually growing herd of aphids. Initially, eating the aphids had been a controversial decision—especially among the aphids. Many of the Senators had believed that the aphids were Alpha Zee citizens, just like the driver ants. But ultimately, the Senate had concluded that only *ants* could be citizens of the hive—all other creatures were either partners or domesticated food providers.

Supplementing the Alpha Zee diet with protein from pupae and aphids worked for six full moons, but ultimately, the aphid birth rate wasn't high enough to sustain the level of consumption, and the Alpha Zee exhausted the pupae in the rival mounds within foraging distance. The loss of these quick and easy sources of protein dramatically changed life in the Alpha Zee hive. When the tribe was nomadic, the hunters had always returned to the bivouac each evening with meat; now flesh was a rare treat, and honeydew was, by far, the Alpha Zee's most frequent meal.

"We can't stay here," President Kadira said simply.

"We're all going—

"—to starve—"

"—to death!" the Secretaries exclaimed.

"Our hunters can travel only an hour on a meal of honey-dew," President Kadira said. "There are other sources of pupae in The Grove, but we can't reach those mounds, because our hunters can't travel that far. We've exhausted the other sources of protein within foraging distance."

"Can't the hunters take aphids with them?" Mallen asked.

"They've tried, but the aphids can't keep up," the President said. "Their legs are too short."

"Why can't some of the workers carry them?"

"You've obviously never heard an aphid squeal," the President said.

"When you pick—"

"—them up they scream—"

"—like banshees," the Secretaries said.

"Non-stop," the President said. "It's maddening."

Lucas Mallen thought for a moment. "I wonder how honeypot ants do it?"

The President and the Secretaries all shrugged. Honeypot ants were experts at collecting, using, and storing honeypot, but no one in the Alpha Zee hive had ever been inside one of their mounds, so they didn't know exactly how all of these tasks were performed.

Mallen said, "The nearest honeypot hive is about forty corons from here. They must have discovered some way to overcome the short-term energy problem."

The President, the Secretaries and the Senate convened for more than an hour. They eventually assigned General Ainsley Walters the task of developing a military plan to attack the Benotobelan honeypot mound. This assault would take a great deal of coordination, because soldiers fed on honeydew couldn't possibly run to the rival hive, engage in combat, and then return home on a single meal. They'd need to be fed along the way.

After spending a full night devising a strategy, General Walters said, "We'll take three platoons of soldiers and 200 aphids. We'll feed on honeydew throughout the trip, and we'll walk slowly so the aphids can keep up. When we get close to the target, we'll eat the aphids. That'll give us the protein we need to sustain ourselves during the battle. After the battle, we'll eat our enemy's pupae, which will give us more than enough energy for the return trip."

When the Alpha Zee soldiers entered the honeypot mound, they easily defeated the rival military and then descended into the deepest chambers, where they discovered a tool far more useful than aphids. Hundreds of honeypot repletes were huddled in a bell-shaped chamber far below the surface. They had overdeveloped social stomachs that could swell to enormous proportions to store honeydew. Their gasters were huge, distended, golden globes, which turned them into living, walking warehouses. So the Alpha Zee soldiers returned home, guiding more than one hundred repletes and carrying thousands of pupae, plus the honeypot Queen, who whimpered at the rear of the phalanx, certain that she would be executed.

"I thought we'd need her to keep producing more repletes," General Walters explained when the President asked about the Queen.

The Alpha Zee Senate made the repletes second-class citizens, and they quickly became the constant companions of the foragers and soldiers out on patrol. They would leave the nest with their gasters full, and return home empty, ready to be filled up again.

Using this mobile food supply, the foragers were able to extend their hunting range, and the military could patrol much larger areas. However, the repletes did not solve all of the Alpha Zee's problems. Now the citizens derived nearly sixty percent of their calories from honeydew, but their bodies had trouble processing so much sugar in their daily diet. Many Alpha Zee citizens grew obese, lethargic, and weak as fat built up under their carapaces, and their muscles atrophied. The soldiers couldn't bite with the same force, the foragers couldn't carry as much weight, and no one seemed to be able to run or fly for any great distance. The ants' waste, which used to be expelled as hard pellets that were easily removed from the hive, was now a runny paste that seeped into the soil and on hot days, the stench spread through the entire mound. The change in diet also caused many ants to develop dementia, violently scrubbing off their scent tags, and sometimes attacking their sisters and brothers. Tens of thousands had died—the stress of the dramatic dietary shift had been too great for them; their bodies had simply shut down.

Lucas Mallen felt responsible for all of these problems. It had been his idea to move into this mound, his idea to form a partnership with the aphids, his idea to raid the honeypot hive. Now he felt it was his duty to save the Alpha Zee by finding a food source that would be predictable, stationary, nutritious, and compatible with their digestive systems. Day after day Mallen climbed up on his high perch studying the vast expanse of The Grove, fruitlessly searching for answers. Finally, the day after a violent wind storm, Lucas Mallen found his answer.

Out in the middle of the pond, he spotted a large, square-headed worker clinging desperately to a broad leaf. Mallen watched for hours as a gentle breeze pushed the leaf back and forth across the surface. Near the end of the day, with the leaf still more than a coron from shore, the ant apparently realized that this was as close as she would get. She put her front legs into the water and paddled hard toward the bank. It was an impressive display of strength and endurance as she slowly dragged herself and the heavy leaf closer to safety. It took nearly an hour, but finally she made it. She stumbled onto the ground, and then, remarkably, turned and pulled the waterlogged leaf onto the sand, before she laid down to rest.

Lucas Mallen watched all of this in amazement. Not even the strongest Alpha Zee soldier could have survived her ordeal—how could this half-dead foreigner be so strong?

What did she eat? Mallen wondered astutely. He knew instantly that whatever she had eaten as her last meal was a fuel that Alpha Zee absolutely had to have. Mallen quickly organized a scouting party to carry him out to the shore.

"Where am I?" the exhausted ant asked when Mallen approached.

"You're just outside of Alpha Zee," Mallen said. He pointed to the huge dark mound rising above the grass in the near distance. He instructed a caretaker to give the ant some food, and the exhausted foreigner greedily sucked down the honeydew. Mallen studied her carefully. He had never seen a worker quite like her. She was gargantuan, nearly as big as an Alpha Zee soldier, and her mandibles were half the size of Mallen's body. Her legs were long and lean, while her torso bristled with muscles. "What's your name?" Mallen asked.

"Pasha," she said. Her breath was so soft that Mallen feared she might die at any moment.

"Where are you from?" he asked desperately. He had to learn the location before she passed away.

"Antistan."

Mallen had never heard of Antistan. "Where is it located?"

Pasha lifted her head and studied the angle of the sun for a moment. She pointed across the pond with her antennae. "Over there." She slumped back to the ground.

Mallen stared out into the distance on the other side of the pond. He wondered how long it would take to walk around the water to get to Antistan. "What do you eat in Antistan?"

"Fungus."

"Fungus?" Mallen had never heard of it. "What is fungus?"

"Like a mushroom."

"Ah …," Mallen said. He'd tasted mushrooms. If that was the type of fungus growing in or around Antistan, then it would be very high in protein—perfect for the Alpha Zee tribe. "Would you like to live with us?" Mallen inquired. "I mean just until we can figure out how to get you back to your home."

She nodded gratefully, and Mallen ordered a group of workers to carry her back to the hive. As they were walking through the corridors of the mound, other citizens started following them, curious about this large stranger who was being carried. Soon the entourage following her had grown to more than 300.

Mallen asked, "So this fungus grows naturally around your hive?"

"Of course not!" screamed a nearby ant gruffly. Mallen turned toward the voice and came face-to-face with a fierce-looking soldier. An angry scar snaked down his face from his forehead, across a milky right eye, and along his cheek. His mandibles were dulled at the ends and pock-marked with scars. "We grow the fungus in deep underground farms."

"We?" Mallen asked. "Who are you?"

"General Paulo Gamba."

"And you're from Antistan also?"

"Yes! This worker can confirm my identity!" The General glared at Pasha with his good eye.

Pasha nodded nervously.

Mallen asked, "Why are you here in Alpha Zee?"

"I was the highest ranking officer in the military, and I was destined to be President of Antistan! But I was falsely accused of murder and forced into exile! I came here because I'd heard that you accepted political refugees."

"But how did you get here?" Mallen asked, wondering if the General had come across the lake, too.

"I walked."

"By yourself?" Mallen didn't know the exact location of Antistan, but he thought it must be too far away for a lone ant to walk.

"Of course, by myself!" Gamba barked. "I told you I was exiled, didn't I?"

"But it's so far away."

"Not for a soldier on fungus rations."

"You said they 'grow' the fungus in Antistan?"

"That's right."

Farming! Lucas Mallen realized that his thinking had been too myopic. Alpha Zee was composed of hunters, gatherers, and, occasionally, scavengers, so Mallen had thought primarily in those terms. But now that he thought about it, he realized that Alpha Zee was already "farming" the aphids to produce honeydew. It was a simple, yet enormous, leap to realize that they could also farm a source of protein.

Lucas Mallen spent a full day talking to Pasha and General Gamba about the fungus-growing process. The following day, Mallen delivered a report to President Kadira and the Secretaries. They all agreed that the fungus sounded like a perfect energy source.

The President ordered General Ainsley Walters to take a small force of soldiers, plus a compliment of repletes on a reconnaissance mission and enter Antistan as scent-camouflaged spies. This was a relatively simple task for the General and his experienced platoon. They crept into the long grass just beyond Antistan's patrolled perimeter, and waited for a lone worker to pass by. Then they grabbed her, stripped away her scent-tag—which meant she could never return to the hive—and used it to concoct their own chemical ID. They entered Antistan without being challenged by the sentries.

When General Walters returned to Alpha Zee a week later, he reported that the fungus *did* exist and it was even *more* valuable than they had hoped.

"We filled our digestive stomachs and our social stomachs with fungus before we left Antistan," General Walters said. "And we were able to make the entire two-day journey without eating again. In fact, I still have some fungus in my social stomach."

Mallen, the President, and the Secretaries stepped forward greedily, presenting their open mouths like desperate pupae. General Walters delivered trophallaxis to each of them, and waited patiently while they slowly chewed the fungus.

"This is delicious!" the President said.

"The best—"

"—meal we've—"

"—ever had!" the Secretaries said.

"Can we grow this here?" Mallen asked for the benefit of the President, the Secretaries and the Senate. He already knew the answer, because he'd spent the past few days being educated by Pasha and former Antistani General Paulo Gamba.

General Walters shook his head. "Growing fungus requires specialized ants with specialized skills." He explained that the leafcutters divided their labor according to a rigid caste system.

Large-headed workers cut down leaves with their powerful mandibles and ferried them back to the mound. Once there, an assembly line of progressively smaller ants cut the leaves into pieces and carried them farther into the narrow corridors of mound. Deep inside a subterranean chamber, the tiniest citizens of Antistan chewed the leaf fragments into a sticky pulp, spread the paste around in a pitch-dark environment, and allowed it to ferment. Within two weeks, fuzzy, white, nutrient-rich mushrooms grew on the fermenting leaves.

"So if we move some of their citizens here," Mallen prompted, "they can use their specialized skills to grow fungus in Alpha Zee."

"They can't move here," General Walters said.

"Why not?" President Kadira asked.

"Yeah," the Secretaries demanded,

"—why—"

"—not?"

"Because fungus production requires a particular type of leaf, which exists in great quantity near Antistan but is non-existent here. Even if the leaf grew here, the entire mound would have to be set up with depots to receive raw leaves, cutting stations to reduce the size of the leaves, transport corridors, and a climate-controlled subterranean farm. It's not possible for us to replicate all of that here."

"So we need a partnership with them," Mallen said. "If you and your troops could travel for two days on a single meal, then this fungus is something we absolutely must have."

The next morning, a war party was assembled, and more than ten thousand ants marched off toward Antistan—Lucas Mallen had to be carried, because he'd grown too large to walk more than a single coron. Nearly one thousand of the ants in the phalanx were fully loaded honeypot repletes.

The Alpha Zee tribe would need to refuel constantly during the journey.

"I thought that we had a strict policy against carrying citizens?" General Walters asked, nodding toward Lucas Mallen.

"We have a policy against carrying *useless* citizens," President Kadira snapped.

When the military finally reached Antistan, the soldiers surrounded the hive, while a small greeting party stepped forward to talk to Antistanti President Keon Nabulung and several members of his Senate.

"Why are you attacking us?" Nabulung asked. "We've done nothing to you."

"Does this look like an attack?" Mallen asked, spreading his front legs innocently.

Nabulung looked at the thousands of Alpha Zee soldiers surrounding the hive. "It looks like a threat."

"We just want to talk to you about your fungus."

"What about it?"

"We want some of it," Mallen stated plainly.

Nabulung chuckled and shook his head. "We're not interested in sharing."

"We could destroy you," Mallen warned. In previous negotiations, the threat of annihilation had always compelled quick agreement from rival hives.

"Yeah?" Nabulung didn't look frightened. He pointed back over his shoulder. "Those are my soldiers, and they'll fight to the death to defend their home—and they'll be fighting with bellies full of fungus, so they can keep at it for hours. Your soldiers ..." He stopped and nodded toward a group of bedraggled Alpha Zee fighters who were lined up to receive food from a replete. "Your soldiers will have to leave the battlefield every half hour to get more honeydew. You won't win."

After several hours of futile debate, the Alpha Zee military left Antistan with no fungus, no partnership agreement, and no hope of ever acquiring the fungus. They were too weak to make credible threats, and they didn't have anything of value to offer Antistan in trade. President Kadira, the Secretaries and the Senate were convinced that the Alpha Zee tribe would have to resume its nomadic life before everyone starved to death. If they returned to their nomadic hunting life, they could eventually come back to Antistan with bellies full of protein and defeat Antistan's army.

But, given the number of Alpha Zee citizens who were now grossly overweight, Mallen thought that there was little hope of reclaiming the hive's previous hunting prowess. The tribe was no longer fit to survive a nomadic life.

Mallen asked the President to give him a few days to confer with General Paulo Gamba and think about the problem. He was convinced that he could come up with a plan to acquire the fungus that Alpha Zee desperately needed.

Mallen was smiling when he finally met with President Kadira, the Secretaries of State, Defense, and Homeland Security (formerly called Bivouac Security), several Senators, and Generals Gant and Walters.

"Antistan needs a new leader," Lucas Mallen said. "Someone who will work with us. Someone we can trust."

The President didn't respond for several moments. "Are you suggesting that we wait until after their next election or coup and then try to negotiate again?"

"I'm suggesting that we look for a candidate *here*," Mallen said. "Former Antistani General Paulo Gamba would make an excellent president."

General Ainsley Walters said, "You're suggesting that we *install* him as the leader?"

General Edmund Gant said, "Our military is wasting away on honeydew. We can't beat their army."

"Would it be easier if Antistan didn't have so many soldiers?" Mallen said slyly.

"Well, duh!" General Edmund Gant said, rolling his eyes.

"What if we could cut their troops in half without endangering ourselves?" Mallen asked.

"How would we do that?" President Kadira asked.

"Yeah," the Secretaries echoed,

"—how would—"

"—we do that?"

Mallen recounted one of the lessons he'd learned from General Gamba. Certain wasps have scent-making ability that can throw an ant mound into absolute chaos. The wasp uses a special chemical to spark a civil war inside the host colony and, while the ants are fighting each other, she marches into the nursery and lays her eggs.

"Are you crazy?" President Kadira asked, his face clouding. "We don't deal with wasps!"

"We *never*—"

"—negotiate—"

"—with terrorists!" the Secretaries said.

"But a wasp can single-handedly cut Antistan's military in half and leave many of the remaining forces injured," Mallen said. "Then, before Antistan recovers, we launch another attack, this time installing our chosen leader."

"But even if we manage to get Gamba in power," President Kadira said, "their Senate still might not approve a fungus deal with us."

"He'll appoint his own Senate," Mallen said.

"Or the military—"

"—might rebel—"

"—against him," the Secretaries said.

"There won't be much of a military left after the civil war," Mallen replied.

"There will be after Antistan's Queen replaces the dead soldiers," President Kadira reminded him.

"She won't replace them," Mallen said simply.

"Why not?" the President asked.

"Yeah—"

"—why—"

"—not?" the Secretaries echoed.

"Because the new President and the new Senate will tell her not to."

The chamber grew still as everyone considered that possibility.

"So our hand-picked President will appoint his own hand-picked Senate, and they'll tell the Queen not to lay any more soldier eggs," President Kadira said slowly. It was a brilliant plan. "But how can we be sure that General Gamba will be loyal to us?"

"I'll move to Antistan as an ambassador to make sure that everything goes according to plan," Mallen said. This would be the opportunity of a lifetime for him. Mallen had a great deal of influence in Alpha Zee, but, ultimately, the President, the Secretaries, and the Senate made all the decisions. They listened to Mallen, but they didn't always follow his suggestions. In Antistan, Mallen could wield real power for the first time in his life. He would use his new-found power to ensure that Alpha Zee got all of the fungus that it needed.

seven

"You can't leave until my position is secure!" Paulo Gamba barked. He was standing just outside Antistan's patrolled perimeter. The day before, the wasp had landed in Antistan and ignited the civil war. Now Alpha Zee Special Forces units were crouched in the grass preparing for the second attack. Gamba's scar changed colors—from placid white to furious red—depending on his mood. At the moment, it was flushed pink.

"Keep your voice down," General Walters said. He stared off into the distance, brooding. Every aspect of this mission made him uneasy. Walters believed that it was one thing to kill an enemy during warfare, but secretly enslaving Antistan by collaborating with a wasp and installing a corrupt dictator seemed like a betrayal of the Alpha Zee's basic identity.

"I can't wait to get back in there," Gamba said, pacing eagerly.

General Walters had known Paulo Gamba only a few days, but it was obvious that the Antistani General was a brutal, egotistical, corrupt, and fundamentally stupid ant. He was barely qualified to *live* in a mound, let alone lead one. He could be counted on to do only one thing—act in his own self interest. But, even then, he was somewhat unpredictable, because he wasn't smart enough to always know what his self-interests were.

Lucas Mallen had adopted the title "Ambassador," and his mission was to keep Gamba pointed in the right direction.

"What's the first thing you're going to do when you get in power, Mr. President?" Ambassador Mallen asked, smiling up at Gamba almost lovingly.

"I'm going to execute every ant who helped expel me from the hive!" Gamba said. He chomped his mandibles together sharply, as if to impress the General and the Ambassador. "I'll line them up and cut them down one-by-one!"

Ambassador Mallen was learning that he could not be too subtle with Paulo Gamba. "Okay," Mallen said. "After *that*, what are you going to do?"

"Then . . .," Gamba said, apparently stumped about the possibilities of Presidential power—other than murder, "I'll call a special meeting of all the citizens . . . and tell them what the new rules are. If anyone disobeys, the consequences will be severe!" He pumped a fist and made a stern face.

General Walters turned to the Ambassador. "You seriously believe that *this* is a good idea?" Walters had lost all respect for Mallen during the past week. Mallen was certainly brilliant, but this plan was too calculated and too devious for Walters' tastes. The unflinching commitment to the Queen's Justice Decree that had compelled Walters to save Lucas Mallen's life on the day of his birth was now stopping him from being an enthusiastic participant in this attack.

Ambassador Mallen sighed. "What I mean," he said in clarification to Paulo Gamba, "is are you going to implement the changes that we talked about?"

"Oh," Gamba frowned. "Yes, of course."

General Walters was tempted to walk away from the entire mission—or kill Paulo Gamba and save everyone the aggravation. Instead, he just huddled under a broad leaf, waiting for dawn to arrive, while cool wind from the Great Plain whistled through the grass. A herd of wildebeests slept fitfully in the distance.

Paulo Gamba bounced from side to side with nervous energy. His bright eye sparkled in the low light, and he grinned, clapping his mandibles together with an annoying clack-clack. "When will we attack?" he asked for at least the tenth time.

General Walters called upon a lifetime of discipline and self-control to keep from slapping Gamba.

"This is gonna be good!" General Gamba said, almost singing. "I can't wait to see the look on Nabulung's face when I kick his ass out of my office."

"What are you going to say to him?" General Walters asked. He knew that Paulo Gamba wouldn't be anywhere near the front line. He'd be safely in the back, moving into the mound only when President Keon Nabulung was dead and the area had been secured.

"I'll tell him he was a stupid jerk to kick me out!" Gamba said. "He should have known that I would come back and take care of him."

"If you want," General Walters suggested, "I could arrange for you to be with the first group of soldiers to enter the mound. That way you could be sure to have a face-to-face with Nabulung and take him down yourself."

"Yeah?" Gamba said uncertainly.

"Absolutely!" General Walters said. "I think it would be quite inspirational to all the troops to see you leading the charge."

"Well, maybe . . .," Gamba said, raising his chin into the air.

"President Gamba," Ambassador Mallen said, "The risk is just too—"

"To hell with the risk!" Gamba stormed. "I'm the rightful President of Antistan! I should be out in front, cutting through the defenses, leading my forces to victory!"

"President Gamba—" Ambassador Mallen started.

"That's the spirit!" General Walters encouraged. "Most leaders are cowards who stand at the back. But you're a true leader in every sense of the word, and I must confess, I have great admiration for you, President Gamba."

Ambassador Mallen rolled his eyes, but Gamba stood tall, swelling under this unexpected praise.

"Okay," the ambassador said, "this is ridiculous. President Gamba, I absolutely forbid you to lead the charge into the mound."

"*Forbid?*" General Walters asked. "A mere Ambassador can't tell a courageous ant like President Gamba that he is forbidden to do anything."

"That's right," Gamba said a little confused. He'd sensed during the past week that General Walters didn't like him, but he couldn't resist the praise.

"President Gamba," Ambassador Mallen said, "Your life is far too valuable to risk in a battle. We need your brain in the Presidential office. We need your leadership, your charisma, and your inspiration. It certainly would be motivating for the troops to see you out front, but what happens if you get injured or killed? Who will lead Antistan? Being a great leader sometimes means that you have to consider the larger implications."

"That's true," Gamba said.

"Of course it is," Ambassador Mallen said. "You're irreplaceable. Let the disposable ants do the fighting."

"You're right," Gamba said, the color in his scar slowly fading. "I must protect myself."

General Walters shrugged. He'd given it a shot.

An hour later, as hazy light shimmered on the horizon, Alpha Zee special-forces units ate several aphids for energy, and then raced out of the foliage and into the Antistani mound.

Ashanti Lehana woke to the sounds of battle and the sharp odor of formic acid. Could there possibly be more fighting? The colony was still reeling from the mysterious attack the day before. This time, Ashanti decided, she had to see the action for herself. She covered her mouth to keep from breathing in poison and pushed toward the surface as waves of her sisters raced deeper into the mound.

"Go *up*, sisters!" she urged. "Go *up!*" Ashanti knew that if even a small portion of Antistan's millions of workers streamed out of the mound together, they could trample any attacking army. But the workers ignored her. They ran away from the fighting, instinctively pulling back to encircle the Queen.

Ashanti continued to push against the crush of bodies and finally reached the surface, which was covered with dead bodies. She recognized the scent of attacking forces. One-on-one battles were being fought all around her. Ashanti had never used her mandibles against another ant, so she wasn't sure what to do. But she stepped forward and sank her jaws into the side of an enemy soldier. He screamed and tried to turn toward her, but an Antistani fighter kept a firm grip on his mandibles. Ashanti lifted her head into the air as if she were hoisting a heavy leaf, and the movement ripped the soldier's body away from his head. She threw the carcass down and darted toward a one-on-one stalemate. Her mandibles didn't have the armor-piercing points that the soldiers had, but the hard labor of foraging had given Ashanti tremendous power. Several times, she found herself isolated on the battlefield and feared that she would be killed, but even though she was engaged in the fighting, the invading soldiers ignored her. She was just a worker, so despite her combative actions, the enemy simply didn't have the intellectual capacity to view her as a member of the army. They ran past her, looking for soldiers to confront. Ashanti fought for hours, developing better and faster technique with each assault. She killed dozens of invaders before the scent of surrender rose from the mound and everyone stopped fighting.

Exhausted, bruised and covered in enemy blood, Ashanti hung her head.

eight

The day after the invasion, President Paulo Gamba stood on a high platform looking down upon the millions of Antistani citizens gathered below him.

"Now that I have assumed the presidency," he said in a loud clear voice. "I will help Antistan reach its full potential." Ambassador Lucas Mallen watched from the corridor as Gamba paced slowly from side to side in an elegant, formal stride. Gamba was a good choice to lead Antistan. He looked and sounded good on the Presidential platform, and with Ambassador Mallen writing his speeches, he would always say the right things.

"The first order of business," Gamba said, "*is* business. For years, we've been a self-sufficient colony. We've avoided trade with others, and usually, we've done okay. But what happened when there was a drought? Or when flooding destroyed our crops? Millions of us starved to death. We can't continue to live like that. So I have a plan that will diversify our economy and protect us from unpredictable natural events."

On that platform, in front of millions, President Paulo Gamba felt confident—he was truly in his element.

"Free trade is the wave of the future," he continued, "and we need to position ourselves to ride it. Colonies all over The Great Plain are engaging in trade that allows them to exchange their products for the products of others. Ants in places we've never heard of will enjoy our delicious fungus, and we'll receive wonderful new foods and other products that we simply can't imagine right now." Gamba paused and studied the crowd. "Are you ready to become the leading fungus distributors on The Great Plain?"

"YES!" the crowd roared back.

"Are you ready to become wealthier than you ever imagined?" Gamba asked.

"YES!" the crowd responded, though the citizens of Antistan did not know the meaning of the word, *wealth*.

"Are you ready to show everyone on The Great Plain just how talented and productive you are?" Gamba asked again.

"YES!" the crowd insisted.

President Gamba left the stage with a sweeping wave and retreated to his private chamber, where Ambassador Lucas Mallen was waiting with a phalanx of Alpha Zee Senators.

"Very well done," Ambassador Mallen said.

President Gamba peered around the chamber, and then brought his good eye back to the Ambassador. "What's she doing here?" Gamba asked, pointing at an Antistani caretaker.

"Her?" Mallen said with a shrug. "This is Miss Olbermeyer. She's serving my dinner." The caretaker produced another bite of fungus from her social stomach; Ambassador Mallen leaned forward to take it from her mandibles and gobbled it down noisily. "How do you think it went?" he asked.

"That's a silly question," Gamba snapped. "My word is law. How did you expect it to go?" The Alpha Zee Senators flinched at his harsh tone, and their fear emboldened Gamba.

"I guess what I meant," Ambassador Mallen asked calmly, "was how did they take it?" He didn't react to President Gamba's aggressive tone. Gamba was the leader of an important colony with a valuable resource; if he wanted to flex his muscles every now and then—especially when he had an audience—Ambassador Mallen would play the role of supplicant.

"I thought," Gamba growled, "that General Walters was supposed to be here to congratulate me?" Gamba desperately wanted to give the General a lecture in front of the Alpha Zee Senators.

"He was called away on another assignment," the Ambassador said.

Gamba paused. "More important than my coronation?"

"Not more important," Ambassador Mallen said, "just different." He realized that Gamba might not be as stupid as everyone thought. He might try to use General Walter's absence as negotiating leverage.

"We're forming a partnership here," Gamba said. "I hope your government isn't already taking me for granted."

"Of course not."

"Because I need to be certain that the Alpha Zee government will follow through on its promises."

"We will follow through."

"It doesn't inspire confidence when General Walters doesn't show up for the very first meeting after I gained control." Gamba glared at the Senators; most of them shuffled uncomfortably, avoiding his eye. "It suggests that I can look forward to more insults in the future."

"As you can see by the ants who are gathered here at the moment, the Alpha Zee Colony is very committed to its relationship with you."

"But General Walters isn't here," Gamba said.

"No, he's not," the Ambassador agreed.

"Maybe my fungus crop isn't so important to the Alpha Zee."

"It's very important."

"Maybe there are other colonies who might want to purchase it."

Ambassador Mallen had let Gamba flex long enough; now it was time to put the restraints back on.

"Come now, President Gamba," he said. He gestured to Miss Olbermeyer who stepped forward to give him another morsel. With a full mouth, he asked smugly, "You don't want me to return to my mound and report that you've made threats, do you?"

"Well," President Gamba squinted, his scar bright red, "It's important to remember that there are other markets."

"Let's be careful with our tone," Ambassador Mallen said. "I'll be sure to tell my president that you're very unhappy that General Walters didn't attend this meeting. I'll be sure to let them know that in the future you expect *and deserve* to be treated with more respect. I'll tell them that you're an important partner, with an important product, and you deserve our fullest attention. Believe me, you'll get what you want. But if I go back and tell them that you've threatened to back out of the agreement, President Kadira is going to take that as a personal affront. Then our military will pay you a visit, but instead of a private meeting with one general, you'll be staring into the faces of fifty thousand Special Forces troops who've come to rip you apart." Ambassador Mallen licked at fungus caught in the corner of his mouth. "Surely, that's not what you want, is it?"

Gamba stared at the Ambassador. He hadn't considered the possibility that Alpha Zee would simply replace him if he tried to use his leverage against them.

"Let's get to the meat of it," Ambassador Mallen said, clarifying the terms of the framework that had been negotiated prior to the attack. "You wanted to be the leader of Antistan, so we've given you that. We're also going to provide military protection for you, so you won't have to waste so many of the Queen's eggs on soldiers. Now that you have control over your Queen's daily scent degree, you can dramatically increase fungus production by telling her to deliver more workers and foragers."

"I know, I know," Gamba said impatiently. "The more workers we have, the more fungus we can produce."

"And those extra workers will create a surplus that can be shipped down to Alpha Zee."

"But," Gamba said, "we lost most of our military in the pseudo civil war and the battle to put me in power."

Ambassador Mallen said, "You won't need one. We'll protect you. Fighting is what we do best. Growing fungus is what Antistan does best. So you focus on growing fungus and we'll focus on destroying your closest rivals and delivering more workers to you as slaves."

President Gamba said, "You're just an Ambassador," he said to Mallen. "How can you guarantee that the Alpha Zee military will destroy my rivals?"

"The same way I guaranteed that we would put you in power," Ambassador Mallen said. He calmly took another bite from the caretaker. He loved the flavor of fungus.

Gamba asked, "What if a migrating colony attacks?" he asked.

"That won't happen," Ambassador Mallen said. "The Alpha Zee will respond very aggressively to any military incursion into The Grove."

"Into the *entire* Grove?" Gamba asked. "That's a big territory."

"We have a big military, and operating on the fuel of fungus, we can cover a lot of ground. There's a bill in the Senate now that would require the military to defend against *every* incursion into The Grove.

"Maybe I should keep growing my military until it passes."

"It will pass," one of the Alpha Zee Senators said with a wink. Gamba winked back, but it was a grotesque gesture, his good eye snapping closed while his milky eye stared out unseeing.

"It will definitely pass," Ambassador Mallen said. "You just need to focus on your workforce."

The next day, Gamba appointed a 100-member Senate made up of ants who were loyal to him. They voted unanimously to change the Queen's pheromone decree. Queen Shasmecka was locked in her deep and heavily guarded chamber and had no direct knowledge of the events that transpired on the surface. She was quite different from Alpha Zee Queen Wenonah. For most of her life, Queen Wenonah had lived a nomadic life; this had given her the opportunity to see many things, visit many regions, and acquire first-hand knowledge of life outside the mound. By contrast, Queen Shasmecka had spent her entire life deep inside the mound—except for her mating flight. She learned of war, famine, drought, disease, and regime change through scent messages communicated to her by her closest caretakers. A daily pheromone decree from the Senate guided her production of eggs to match the colony's changing needs. If several military divisions were killed in a war, the Queen would lay more soldier eggs. If a flood washed away thousands of workers, she'd lay more worker eggs. Farmers, foragers, and virgin female caretakers made up the rest of her daily brood. The Queen was merely a birthing machine; she obeyed the Senate's decrees without question.

nine

Fungus was transported from Antistan to Alpha Zee along a system of relay points set up at sixteen-coron intervals. It took roughly four hours to carry a load of fungus from one depot to the next, and there, the load was handed off to a rested ant, who took it the next four hours of the route. In this manner, thick bolls of cottony fungus reached Alpha Zee every morning. At first, the fungus was carefully rationed to ensure that each full-blooded citizen received an ample share. But soon the daily import was so large that even the second-class citizens could get their fill.

Fungus was a magic elixir that allowed the foragers to work twelve-hour days without growing weary. The Senators could negotiate with more clarity, the military could conquer enemies farther away, and the Queen could deliver more eggs. Almost overnight the Alpha Zee changed from a hive languishing on a diet of honeydew into a super-efficient, super-organism, raising ever-larger herds of aphids, and controlling ever-larger swatches of land.

"It's not enough for the military to protect just the hive, or even the area immediately around the mound," Ambassador Mallen said during a Senate debate. He had returned from Antistan to argue in favor of The Grove Protection Act. "We need a perimeter that will extend to the boundaries of The Grove."

"Exactly what do you mean by the *boundaries* of The Grove?" General Ainsley Walters asked.

Ambassador Mallen said, "Every blade of grass, every flower, every bush, and every tree, from edge to edge."

"That's a perimeter of 400 corons and a total area of more than 10,000 square-corons!"

"I know the dimensions, General."

"Why would we ask our soldiers to defend such an impossibly large territory?"

"To protect our hive and our way of life."

General Walters studied the Ambassador for a moment. "When we were a migratory tribe, we patrolled a one-coron perimeter around the bivouac and that provided enough security. Since moving into this hive, we've defended an area of 25 square corons, and that has kept us safe. Expanding to protect 10,000 square corons is an enormous and unnecessary leap."

"Our economy has changed," Mallen said. "Our aphids eat grass and flowers, and the workers of Antistan use leaves to grow their fungus. Those are the same foods that herds of wildebeest and antelopes consume when they migrate through this territory, so we have to protect those grazing and foraging areas."

The citizens of Alpha Zee loved the taste of fungus, and they now understood that they couldn't live without it, but they still weren't convinced that The Grove Protection Act, with its enormous military commitment, was necessary to protect their fungus import. President Kadira calculated that if the citizens weren't motivated to defend grazing areas for economic reasons, then he would shift the conversation to a topic that was sure to get their attention.

"It's more than other creatures eating our food," President Kadira said. "A herd could trample our mound and kill the Queen!"

The Senators gasped.

"With all due respect, Mr. President," General Walters said. "That's a pretty bold statement. As a general in our army, I am directly responsible for the physical security of our mound, and I know that even if the heaviest mammal stepped directly on our hive, the Queen is so far below the surface that no harm could possibly come to her."

The President glared. "*You* may be willing to gamble with the Queen's life, but I'm not." He couldn't believe that General Walters had openly challenged him in front of the Senate.

"With all due respect, Mr. President," General Walters continued, fearlessly. "Mammals don't trample ant mounds, because they don't want our soldiers climbing up their legs and biting their most sensitive places. Except for anteaters, a mammal's instinct for self-preservation will keep him away from us."

Ambassador Mallen said, "If we have the *capacity* to defend ourselves, why should we sit back and *trust* the self-preservation instinct of mammals? How can we assume that all of them are sane and will act in predictable ways?"

"We have to make some reasonable assumptions," General Walters said, "because the alternative is foolishly trying to defend *every coron* of The Grove."

The President directed his comments to the Senate. "The way this would work is that we would position platoons of soldiers in bivouacs throughout The Grove so that they can respond quickly to any incursion."

General Walters shook his head. "If they're living permanently away from our hive, then they won't be able to communicate with their generals."

The President looked at General Walters quizzically. "These are *your* soldiers. They're highly trained, highly decorated troops. Surely, we can trust them to make a few decisions about how best to deal with threats to our society."

General Walters said, "That's not how our military is designed to work. We don't rely on *trust*. We rely on transparency and oversight. Our soldiers need orders, a chain of command, and ultimately, civilian oversight from the Senate."

"I'm surprised that a soldier of your experience is so distrustful of your fellow service members," Ambassador Mallen said.

General Walters ignored Mallen's comment, "Plus, in order to adequately defend every coron of The Grove, we'd need the Queen to deliver three times as many soldiers as we currently have at the same time that the death rate of soldiers will increase dramatically. Living in bivouacs near our enemies will be very dangerous for them."

"That's the price—"

"—that must be paid—"

"—to ensure our freedom," the Secretaries said.

The debate continued for several weeks without resolution. Ambassador Mallen, had to be ferried back and forth from Antistan, and he was growing frustrated.

Ultimately, a single, chance event decided the issue in favor of a larger military. On a morning near the end of the dry season, low rumbles vibrated through the mound, signaling the approach of a herd.

Though the President didn't have the authority to order soldiers to defend The Grove against *all* incursions, he could send the troops out by executive order on a case-by-case basis, and this strategy seemed to be working. Most herds had begun to avoid The Grove despite its lush garden of grass, flowers, and weeds.

General Ainsley Walters led the troops out in the direction of the herd. Although he disagreed with the policy of defending every coron of The Grove, he'd never argued against any particular defensive effort. He was a soldier, and when a threat existed, he served valiantly and faithfully.

The dry season had parched The Great Plain, but the plants in The Grove had a private water supply that protected them from the general shortage. Tall stalks and fresh blooms stretched their roots toward the pond and swayed in the gentle breeze.

Wildebeests hacked and coughed in the distance, tempted by the clear blue water in the center of The Grove, but not yet thirsty enough to take the risk. This late in the season, most water holes had been tramped and sloshed by bathing elephants, who soaked up the dregs like sponges and marched off with mud-caked hides, leaving behind barely damp soil that the sun cracked and fissured. But even the elephants, with their thick hides, hadn't ventured into The Grove.

A herd of migrating impalas—most with skin stretched so tightly across their starved ribs that they appeared, from a distance, to be striped like zebras—marched with their heads down, tearing at the overgrazed grass with sharp teeth.

A hungry and frustrated six-month-old male near the edge of the pack stamped his hooves; puffs of dust rose into the sky. He licked his dry lips and inched closer to The Grove.

By then, tens of thousands of Alpha Zee soldiers had reached the perimeter.

"Up here!" General Walters urged, leading a group of soldiers up a tree.

The young impala crept closer to the grass. He lifted his nose in the air and savored the sweet smell of the stalks. No other member of the impala herd had come near the verdant plants—his instincts told him that The Grove must be dangerous. But hunger pains wracked his empty stomach and drove him closer. He crept forward, keeping his legs tensed.

He strained with his neck and stretched his long lips out to grasp a weed, ripping it from the soil, keeping his eyes trained on the near distance. At the first sign of a predator, he would spring away with a high kick and dart across the plain. But nothing moved in the grass. His jaw turned lazy circles, and he sighed at the delicious taste. He didn't notice that the stalk was teeming with ants. His teeth crushed dozens of soldiers, but many more raced into his mouth and clamped their sharp mandibles down on the soft tissue of his lips, gums, tongue, and cheek. The impala shook his head and flicked his ears. He spat out the long weed, but the pain didn't go away. He bleated and stamped his feet. In confusion, he turned in a wobbly circle that put him farther into The Grove.

Alpha Zee soldiers raced up the impala's legs and pinched his thick hide, but the animal barely noticed; the ants tearing at the flesh in his mouth had captured his full attention. He bleated and ran toward a tree, rubbing his face against the rough bark. He didn't notice that the trunk was covered with Alpha Zee soldiers. General Walters led the charge onto the impala's head. He went straight for the impala's left eye, while others climbed into the right eye. The impala blinked and ran in desperate circles. On General Walters' command, the soldiers reared back and drove their mandibles into the impala's tough eyeballs.

"Poison!" General Walters ordered. Each of the ants pumped a full load of formic acid into the puncture wounds. A platoon of Alpha Zee soldiers stabbed through the impala's eardrums, while other ants crawled deep into the animal's sinuses. The impala sneezed a dozen times and issued a high, whining bleat that echoed off the hard trunks of the trees and drew the attention of the entire herd. He leaped into the air, thrashing his body from side to side, kicking his hind legs. Now blind, he darted forward. One of his hooves came down hard on the northern edge of the Alpha Zee mound, killing thousands of ants. He crashed into a tree. His left shoulder cracked. When he struggled back to his feet, one leg dangled uselessly. The herd of impalas seemed to flinch as the screaming three-legged young animal hurdled blindly into another tree. He crumpled to the ground, bleeding from every orifice.

A pack of hyenas with their noses high in the wind trotted toward the kill, scattering the herd of impalas in a thunderous panic. The hyenas ran back and forth at the edge of the tall grass, barking wildly but not advancing as blood drained out of the impala's young body. Vultures, drawn by the scent, landed and skulked nearby, keeping a careful distance from the hyenas *and* the ants. Soon a pride of lions approached, driving away the vultures and scaring off the frustrated hyenas, who growled and nipped, but retreated. The lions settled on the low turf of the prairie and waited, panting in the midday sun.

The ants could not eat the impala—not all of it. Workers tore at the animal's flesh and carried as much protein as they could back to the mound, but the Alpha Zee couldn't possibly store the entire animal.

"See?" Ambassador Mallen said, surveying the damaged section of the mound. "Now can you see why we need The Grove Protection Act?"

"The impala stepped on the mound *because* of our military attack rather than in spite of it," General Walters said. "If we hadn't initiated contact, he would have nibbled from the edge of The Grove and left. Instead, we blinded him, caused him to panic, which led directly to his accidentally trampling our hive."

"This is exactly the type of *accident* that could be prevented if mammals were not permitted to enter The Grove at all!" Mallen insisted.

The Senate agreed with the Ambassador. The Grove Protection Act passed unanimously, and the Queen's daily scent decree changed. Previously, fifteen percent of her eggs were committed to new soldiers, but now that a bigger force was needed to defend The Grove, thirty-five percent of her larvae would be devoted to the military.

"Now," Ambassador Mallen asked, after the legislation passed, "how are we going to get this carcass off of our grazing areas? This dead animal is a potential ecological disaster. It will poison the soil. Deadly bacteria will filter into the pond, and everything in The Grove will be contaminated."

"What can we do?" President Kadira asked.

"We should let the lions have the body," Mallen said.

"How do we do that?" the President asked.

"We give them a signal," Ambassador Mallen said.

The workers and soldiers, who had covered the animal like a thick red blanket, made a big show of backing away. They continued to retreat making it clear that they were giving up the corpse. After a brief interval, the so-called king of the jungle inched forward to grab the carcass and drag it off the Alpha Zee's land. That lion was the last mammal ever to enter The Grove.

A few days later, Ambassador Lucas Mallen was summoned to the Queen's chamber, where he received the Pheromone of Honor—the highest praise any ant could receive.

Your brain and your insights have completely transformed our society, Queen Wenonah said. *You've improved our birthrate, taught us how to thrive in one location, and created a relationship with Antistan that delivers this wonderful fungus every day. You are our most cherished citizen.*

She attached the pheromone to the base of his antennae, where it slowly seeped into his skin and into his scent glands.

From that day forward, the Pheromone of Honor became Ambassador Mallen's dominant scent. It earned him unparalleled and unprecedented status in the hive.

"And to think," Mallen bragged to everyone he met, "I was nearly put to death at birth because I had no mandibles."

ten

The low sun hung over Ashanti Lehana's shoulder as she stumbled back to Antistan under a triangular sail of green. The leaf in her jaws gave her shadow a long angular head like a preying mantis. It was her twelfth load of the day, a record even for her, and she thought she might get in one or two more before nightfall.

Ashanti approached an Antistani soldier, the first she'd encountered in hours, and paused. She didn't know how he would react to her. More than a month had passed since Paulo Gamba had gained control of the government, and she had heard that his soldiers had bullied workers and a few had even committed murder for sport. Ashanti watched the soldier closely, but he ignored her. She passed him, then stopped, dropped her heavy load and turned back toward him.

"Where's the rest of the military?" she asked. Ashanti had become a question machine. Every day she posed more queries, and every reply produced still more questions.

The fighter looked at her with half-closed eyes. He shrugged. "Down the path."

Ashanti looked in both directions. She didn't see any other soldiers. "I just came about three corons in that direction," she pointed, "and I didn't see anyone." She looked down the trail, pointing again, "and I don't see anyone there either. Usually, there's at least one soldier every eighth of a coron, but now you're the only one in sight."

The soldier yawned.

Ashanti studied him. She had only half an hour before the horizon eclipsed the sun. "Did we lose that many fighters in the wars?" Ashanti asked. "The Queen must be replenishing our military right now."

"Must be," the soldier said.

"But what if someone attacks us?"

The soldier shook his head. "We have Alpha Zee protection."

"The Alpha Zee?" Ashanti said. "They're the ones who attacked us in the first place!"

"They're protecting us," the soldier said.

"Well, where are they?" Ashanti asked.

"Out there," the soldier pointed. "They have a perimeter set up. No one can get in."

Ashanti stared into the thick vegetation. She wondered how far out the perimeter extended. Earlier, she'd marched for nearly an hour without crossing any discernable defensive positions. She puzzled over this for a moment, but the long shadows told her that she didn't have much time. She sighed and staggered sideways before getting the load re-settled in her mandibles.

eleven

A thin, nearly translucent ant crawled into Ambassador Lucas Mallen's chamber in the Antistani mound. The ant stood still for a long moment as if catching her breath from the effort of her brief walk from the corridor into his room. On Mallen's orders, a worker had carried her from the Queen's distant quarters up to Mallen's door.

"Hasina Binsaw, my old friend!" Ambassador Mallen greeted her with a hug and a kiss on the cheek. "How are you?" This was the tiny ant who had been ferried into Antistan aboard the wasp.

"What's that smell?" Hasina asked.

"What smell?"

"The funny odor."

Mallen sampled the air. "I'm not picking up anything."

She waved her antennae in his direction. "It's you."

"Oh that," Mallen said, blushing. "I received the Pheromone of Honor from Queen Wenonah. I keep forgetting that I have it."

"You forget that you smell like a rotting dung beetle?"

"Don't be ridiculous," Mallen stammered.

"I feel dizzy," Hasina said. She appeared to be on the verge of passing out.

"Is there anything you need?" Ambassador Mallen inquired as if he personally would attend to her requests. "Additional rations, more space? Anything at all." Mallen loved being an

Ambassador. He had real power, and he felt as though he had his own laboratory in which to experiment with different policies.

"I'm fine," Hasina said.

Ambassador Mallen's face creased in a thin smile. "Tell me about the Queen."

Hasina hated that condescending smile. "She's fine."

"Oh, Hasina," he teased with a weary shake of his head, "you always were the reticent one. I know she's fine, but what I want to know is how productive she is."

"How should I know?"

"Come now, Hasina," Ambassador Mallen said. "You've been with her every moment for more than a month, and you've lived with other queens. How does she compare?"

Hasina was a parasite of the species *Tetramorium caespitum*. Her concave body fit perfectly atop the abdomen of the Antistani queen. Once in position, Hasina's own abdomen swelled with eggs, and she produced a litter whose scent matched Antistan's colonial odor so expertly that the caretakers fed Hasina as if she were the Queen and took her eggs without question. Her parasitic offspring produced nothing, built nothing and contributed nothing to the Antistani community. They merely attached their concave bodies to the backs of caretakers and consumed meals whenever they had the opportunity.

Hasina shrugged. "She's patient."

"Patient?" Ambassador Mallen asked, losing *his* patience. "I ask you how she is, and you tell me 'patient'? Who cares how patient she is! How many eggs a minute is she producing?"

Hasina found it interesting that as the Ambassador achieved greater power, his sense of humor became progressively smaller.

"Two or three."

"Two or three?" Ambassador Mallen's voice whined like a locust's chirp, and his mouth glistened as if he'd just taken a feeding. "Well, which is it? Two? Or three?"

Like it mattered.

"Three, I think."

"Three, you think?" Ambassador Mallen laughed. He shook his head. "Well, I guess that's going to have to be good enough. One egg every twenty seconds." He chuckled again. "That's pretty productive, isn't it?"

Hasina shrugged. Lucas Mallen had discovered her in Alpha Zee, shortly after he'd learned about the existence of parasites. He'd instructed the caretakers to scrub hard across the Queen's back every evening. Executing this policy, the caretakers had dislodged Hasina Binsaw, and once she had been separated from her host, her scent had reverted to its original pheromone. She'd been imprisoned and scheduled for trial. The punishment for anyone found guilty of parasitism was death. But Mallen had proposed a deal that would save her from execution. He wanted her to enter Antistan with a wasp, and position herself to monitor the Queen's activities.

In his chamber, with the Pheromone of Honor billowing off his skin, Mallen said, "I need to know exactly what the Queen is doing."

Hasina sat down and closed her eyes. "Why?" she murmured.

"Why?" Mallen snapped. "Because I saved you! That's why!" Then for emphasis, he said, "You're a *parasite*." He packed the word with venom. "The only thing you're good at is mooching off other ants."

Hasina said, "I'm still trying to figure out what makes you less of a parasite than me."

"I am certainly *not* a parasite," Ambassador Mallen huffed.

"I negotiate mutually beneficial trade agreements." He ran one of his front legs across the top of his bald head.

"Mutually beneficial?" Hasina worked the phrase around in her mouth. "What's the benefit for Antistan?"

"They get Alpha Zee protection."

"Protection that you forced them to take."

"We didn't force—" Ambassador Mallen exhaled heavily. "I'm not going to argue with a parasite."

"Why do you need to know a breakdown of the Queen's egg distribution?"

"So that we can make sure President Gamba is complying with the terms of the agreement."

"Why don't you just ask him?"

Ambassador Mallen chewed the inside of his cheek. "Look, if you're unhappy with our arrangement, let me know, and you'll be homeless within hours. Otherwise, tell me *exactly* what the Queen is laying."

Hasina Binsaw sighed and said, "lots of workers."

Ambassador Mallen waited. "And?"

"And what?"

"And what else?" he screamed.

"Some caretakers."

Ambassador Mallen took a slow breath. "What percentage are soldiers?"

"I don't know," Hasina said. "Not much."

"What's not much? Five percent? Ten percent?"

"More like fifteen or twenty."

Ambassador Mallen threw back his head and stared at the ceiling. "You're lying."

Hasina Binsaw rolled her eyes.

"You know what I do every day, Hasina?" Ambassador Mallen asked.

"Live the life of a highly placed parasite?"

"No!" Mallen hissed. "I monitor situations and gather information. I attend the Antistani Senate every day, and I've smelled the decree to the Queen with my own antennae. I know what it says. I know that she's on a five percent military production schedule."

"If you're so sure, why bother having these silly meetings?" Hasina started moving toward the door.

"You're saying Gamba is pulling some sort of trickery?" Ambassador Mallen asked. "That somehow between the Senate chamber and the Queen, he's increasing the percentage?"

Hasina didn't respond. She walked outside and hitched a ride back down to the Queen's chamber.

The next morning, Antistani sentries spotted soldiers from a rival colony racing toward the mound. President Paulo Gamba ordered all of his troops to the battlefield, and he watched from a high perch as his woefully small band of fighters was cut down.

Gamba turned toward Ambassador Mallen, who was reclining luxuriantly in the President's chamber.

"How could this happen?" Gamba thundered.

Ambassador Mallen shrugged his puny shoulders and grinned smugly as he watched President Gamba.

"Your army was supposed to protect us!" President Gamba's scar was white with fear. Even though he'd been secretly increasing the size of his army, his troops were no match for the enormous force swarming out of the grass.

"We'll protect you," Ambassador Mallen said, "but you weren't moving fast enough on the military reduction. We had to take a calculated risk."

"That," Gamba screamed, pointing outside, "is not a risk! It's suicide! They'll be on top of us in minutes!"

Ambassador Mallen shook his head. "No they won't."

Gamba turned away from the carnage below him. "What do *you* know about military strategy?"

"The goal of this operation is to get rid of your remaining forces. You didn't put your Queen on the program that you were supposed to, so we had to intervene. What were you telling her? Fifteen, twenty percent soldiers?"

Gamba blanched. How did Ambassador Mallen know the percentages of the Queen's production schedule?

"You've seen the scent decrees," President Gamba said without conviction.

"Yes, and I know that you change them after they leave the Senate."

Gamba raised his chin in the air. "Well, I have to maintain some sort of military force. Surely, you don't expect me to be completely defenseless." Outside, the enemy soldiers raced toward the mound.

Suddenly, fluttering shadows zoomed across President Gamba's face. He looked up and saw thousands of winged Alpha Zee fighters dipping out of the sky. The Alpha Zee military, powered by a steady diet of fungus, was the most dominant fighting force on The Great Plain. They landed in front of the enemy, snapping their razor-sharp mandibles open and closed. The attacking ants turned as one and sprinted away. The Alpha Zee soldiers chased them into the underbrush. All that remained on the battlefield were the dead bodies of President Gamba's soldiers. His entire army had been destroyed.

President Gamba turned away from the carnage, scowling.

"You can start over now," Ambassador Mallen continued. "The Queen can dedicate three percent of the eggs for soldiers, solely for internal policing. If you violate this agreement again, the consequences will be far more severe. Do we understand each other?"

Gamba glowered at the obese little ant.

"As regards the fungus deal," Mallen continued, "we'll now take thirty percent of the gross."

"The gr . .gr . . gross," President Gamba stuttered.

"Considering that we've helped you dramatically increase your labor force, and the Alpha Zee military is keeping you and your citizens alive, thirty percent is quite fair."

Gamba's scar turned pink. "The citizens will revolt," he said, as if his constituents were his chief concern.

"No, they won't," Ambassador Mallen said. "You just have to convince them that this is a change for the better."

"What if I can't convince them?"

Ambassador Mallen shrugged slowly. "Then we might have the wrong ant leading Antistan."

twelve

President Paulo Gamba stood on his platform halfway up the east wall of the great chamber. He looked over the throng of workers and caretakers assembled below him. With all the slaves the Alpha Zee military had delivered from defeated mounds, the chamber was crowded with more ants than ever before. There was no question that Antistan could produce more fungus, but President Gamba noted ruefully that he did not have a single soldier in the audience. Despite Ambassador Mallen's assurances, President Gamba did not believe that he could maintain control over his population without a military. But there was little he could do about it now. In order to guarantee his position as President of Antistan, Gamba had to compel the members of his colony to work even harder.

The crowd below President Gamba tittered nervously. There was a great deal of confusion in Antistan. The citizens didn't understand why their military was gone, why the colony had adopted so many slaves from other mounds, why juvenile ants were being put to work younger than ever before, why everyone was working more hours every day, and why they were receiving less food even though they seemed to be more productive. The lack of information gave rise to rumors that grew more vicious with every turn.

"I know that many of you," President Gamba began, believing that he had to tell his citizens something to keep them under control, "are wondering about the state of our military." He coughed to suppress his own fears. "I have decided that we should not waste our precious resources on an army. We all know that soldiers eat a lot of food, but they don't do anything to help the colony between wars."

The crowd nodded. They all knew that soldiers did no work.

"The protection of the Alpha Zee military allows us to concentrate our efforts on collecting leaves, growing fungus, and building the biggest and best leafcutter society The Great Plain has ever seen!"

A chant started in the crowd, and it quickly spread from the front of the chamber to the back:

"NO MORE MILITARY! GROW MORE FUNGUS!"
"NO MORE MILITARY! GROW MORE FUNGUS!"
"NO MORE MILITARY! GROW MORE FUNGUS!"

All ants on The Great Plain were the same: Though few had individual egos, they all had tremendous tribal pride; they needed to hear themselves complimented; they needed to believe that their hive was the best of all the hives. The most talented leaders were those who understood that scents and chants were the fuel that ran the colony—give the workers the right scent, and they'd believe anything; give them a good chant, and they'd accomplish anything.

After the chant died down, Ashanti's friends talked about the President's speech.

"He's right," Justine Ricardo said. "The soldiers consume a lot of resources, but they do no work at all, and they're horribly abusive."

"Did you know," Laura Mejia said with an air of certainty as if someone in the colony actually kept records of mortality rates and causes of death, "that our military has killed more Antistani workers over the years than famine and disease?"

"I believe it," Justine said, shaking her head. "They're savages."

"Just terrible, aggressive, wasteful souls," Laura said sadly.

Ashanti listened to her friends with growing impatience. She heard too much of herself in their voices. Just a few months ago, she would have accepted everything President Gamba had said without hesitation because she'd always been a loyal and faithful worker who would never think to question her government. But now, Ashanti saw through the President's gauzy rhetoric. The Alpha Zee tribe had manipulated President Gamba, and all of Antistan would suffer under the pressure to produce more fungus.

When the chanting had started, Ashanti's natural instinct was to join in. But somehow, she knew that she couldn't chant with her sisters. It took great effort, but Ashanti had managed to fight off the urge, and she stood alone in the sea of voices, listening to her brothers and sisters and truly hearing them for the first time. Her rebellious silence somehow made her immune to the euphoria of the chant, and her mind stayed clear while her fellow citizens became too giddy to think, and too intoxicated to object.

"In light of the Alpha Zee's increased commitment to our defense," President Gamba continued, "I've given them permission to sell a slightly larger share of the fungus crop on the open market."

"A larger share?" Ashanti asked, though she had clearly heard the President's words.

"A *slightly* larger share," Justine clarified.

"That's okay," Laura said. "We can give them a little more, because when it comes to fungus, we're the best of the best!"

"THE BEST OF THE BEST!" A few ants nearby chanted.

"Now that we don't have a military to feed," President Gamba continued, "we're more efficient than ever. We have an opportunity to trade our excess fungus for other products and services."

"He's got a point," Justine said.

"We *are* more efficient," Laura agreed.

Trading it for what? Ashanti wondered. She considered the long hours she spent in the fields; she was motivated solely by her desire to help the colony and protect the Queen. As far as she knew, no one in the mound had ever wanted or needed to *trade* for anything. They lived together as a family, sharing their resources according to their needs. But now, they were supposed to generate a surplus that would produce something called *profit*, which was a concept Ashanti was only just beginning to understand. She realized that her initial assumptions about her fellow ants may have been wrong. She had always assumed that her brothers and sisters were every bit as dedicated to the tribe as she was. But as she studied President Gamba on his high perch, she realized that there might be ants who acted in their own self-interest without regard for the hive. In that case, the colony's greatest strength—the loyalty of its citizens—could also be its greatest weakness, because loyal citizens were unlikely to challenge a leader who abused his authority.

"So the Alpha Zee," President Gamba continued, "will take thirty percent of the fungus."

Ashanti gasped.

"That's a lot," Justine said. She looked at her friends, trying to decide if she should worry.

"But we can afford it," Laura said. "We're expert farmers. We're the best of the best!"

"That's right!" Justine agreed. "We can always grow more!"

President Gamba said, "Alpha Zee workers will ferry thirty percent of the daily fungus harvest to their mound."

"Do you mean," someone in the audience asked tentatively, "they'll take thirty percent *before* each of us gets our daily meal?"

A gasp ran through the audience. It hadn't occurred to most of them that the rations that kept them alive might be in jeopardy. During the past few months, the Alpha Zee had always taken a percentage of the fungus *surplus*. After the Queen had been fed, after every Antistani citizen had eaten, after the pupae took their share, after food was stored away to cover rations for a week, only then did the Alpha Zee take its portion of the crop.

The President cleared his throat and said, "Yes, they're going to take their percentage from the gross, but it's very reasonable considering what we're getting." He had to raise his voice to be heard over the tittering crowd. "We're getting top of the line production strategies, development of our infrastructure, and the protection of the most powerful military on The Great Plain. No one will ever attack us. Even herds of wildebeests, zebras, and antelopes won't graze near us because of the Alpha Zee military."

"We never needed them to keep the mammals away before!" Ashanti said venomously. "He's turning us into slaves for the Alpha Zee!"

Justine and Laura looked at each other.

"Don't be ridiculous," Justine said.

"Thirty percent of the gross does seem like a lot," Laura conceded.

Ashanti knew instinctively that no matter how much protection the Alpha Zee military offered and no matter what Antistan received in trade, thirty percent of the gross was far too much to surrender. Ashanti studied President Gamba and noticed that his gait lacked its usual swagger, and his good eye seemed to flit uncomfortably. In his posture, she could see that he too believed the contract with the Alpha Zee was bad for Antistan, and this thought filled Ashanti with joy. Maybe

President Gamba *did* have the best interests of the hive in mind. Maybe the Alpha Zee had tricked him. If so, there was still hope of undoing the damage. Now that Ashanti had a sense of her own individuality, she sympathized with President Gamba. She realized that it must be lonely to be the leader of a colony, making so many important decisions and having no one to turn to for advice. It would be easy to get bullied by a bigger colony. But what if Gamba knew that the workers were behind him? What if he knew that the citizens would support him if he stood up to Alpha Zee? Ashanti's heart beat faster as the possibilities raced through her mind. Maybe there was something that *she* could do about all of this.

When the oration ended, Ashanti stayed behind as her brothers and sisters filed out.

"Aren't you coming?" Justine asked.

"I need to run a quick errand," Ashanti said. They shrugged and left with the rest of the crowd. Once the massive chamber was empty, Ashanti began the long climb up to the Presidential suite. When she finally arrived, she fidgeted outside his doorway, trying to decide on exactly what she would say to President Gamba. After a moment, she heard him speaking to someone inside.

"I am the President of this colony!" he said, "And I demand that you show me proper respect!"

Ashanti had never heard the President use that tone of voice. She wondered what citizen had dared to upset him, and whether she would be the next target of his wrath. She was just a worker, a forager. Who was she to approach the President with her ideas? She turned to leave, but after a few steps, she turned back. She couldn't leave; her love for the colony was too strong. She had spent her entire life following orders, never questioning any policy. But now that she had become a thinking ant, she felt a duty to use her mind to help the colony. She *had* to talk to the President. She had to let him know that the citizens would support him if he turned against the Alpha Zee.

Ashanti set her chin and marched through the doorway. President Gamba was yelling at a massive Alpha Zee general. The soldier was twice the size of the President yet he endured the verbal assault with docile indifference.

"I want you to *apologize!*" President Gamba's scar was almost maroon. "I want you to get down before me and apologize!"

The General didn't respond, but a faint smile played across his face. Ashanti was shocked to see a measure of kindness in the General's face. Most soldiers had only two moods: boredom and anger, and they vacillated between them with deadly quickness. But this Alpha Zee general had a gentleness about him that made Ashanti feel that, despite his bristling power, he was the least dangerous ant in the room.

"Get that smile off your face!" Gamba said.

The General continued to stare back with the same enigmatic expression.

Gamba turned away and said, "Ambassador Mallen, I thought you said he was supposed to—" He stopped when he noticed Ashanti in the doorway.

"What?" He spat at her.

The sudden shift caught Ashanti off guard.

"I wondered . . . if I could . . . talk to you for a moment?"

President Gamba glared at her with his good eye. No citizen had ever come to his chamber to talk to him. No workers, no soldiers, no members of the Senate—no one. He issued orders and the citizens followed them; he wasn't sure how to respond to this unprecedented interruption.

"About what?"

Ashanti cleared her throat and looked from the Alpha Zee general to Ambassador Mallen and back to President Gamba. "I wondered . . . if . . . if I could talk to you *privately*."

"She wants to talk, *and* she wants privacy," Ambassador Mallen said, winking at the President. "Maybe she wants to do more than *talk*."

There was no sex in Antistan. The Queen had been inseminated years ago, which allowed her to produce eggs without further male contact. The workers and soldiers were sterile, and the virgin females, who attended to the Queen, came into heat just once a year when they left the mound to find mates and start colonies of their own. The workers of Antistan were not even aware of the concept of sex, so the hidden meaning of Ambassador Mallen's comment was beyond the range of Ashanti's imagination.   President Gamba chuckled without conviction and said, "Yeah, maybe she does want to do more than talk." Ashanti could tell from his tone that he could not imagine what Ambassador Mallen thought they might do.

"Well, I'm not leaving," Ambassador Mallen said. "And neither is General Walters. If she wants to get frisky, she's gonna have to do it in front of us."

"Get *frisky*?" Ashanti asked. The Ambassador seemed to be speaking another language.

"What do you want?" Gamba barked.

Ashanti shifted on her feet, looking back and forth at the three ants. Maybe President Gamba wasn't in the right mood to hear that the workers were behind him. But she was there, so she might as well say what she'd come to say. She took a deep breath. "I wanted to talk to you about the deal with the Alpha Zee."

"Yeah?" Gamba scowled.

"I don't . . . I don't think it's fair."

Ambassador Mallen burst out laughing. His reedy voice vibrated like the rumble of an annoying horse fly. He howled and howled, doubling over, rolling onto his back and kicking his legs into the air.

"She wanted . . .," Ambassador Mallen said, trembling. "She wanted privacy . . . because . . . she . . . doesn't think—" laughter shook his frame. "She doesn't think—" he started again, "that the . . . deal is . . . fair!"

Ashanti's face flushed hot. "That's exactly what I think!" she said, standing tall and blowing air from her cheeks. The Ambassador continued to laugh at her, and Ashanti felt herself getting angry.

He caught his breath and sighed several times, shaking his head and chuckling quietly. "Tell me something, President Gamba," Ambassador Mallen said, wiping tears from his eyes. "Do all your workers spend their time second-guessing you, or do some of them actually *work?*"

Ashanti's mouth fell open at this insult.

"What's your name?" President Gamba demanded. His scar was crimson.

"Ashanti Lehana," she said defiantly. For most of her life, Ashanti had never felt individual pride. She had never considered whether she was better, stronger, or more efficient than her peers. But now she felt a burst of ego. She wasn't just an ant; she was Ashanti Lehana, a hard working, intelligent ant, who was willing to do anything to defend her tribe. Ambassador Mallen's derisive laughter only hardened her resolve.

"Well, Ashanti Lehana," Gamba said, deciding that she was a suitable target for his frustrations, "guess what your insubordination has earned you?"

"What?" Ashanti asked.

"A death sentence," President Gamba said merrily. He advanced on her with his mandibles braced open.

Ashanti was too stunned to move. She'd come to the President's chamber to tell him that she and the other workers were on his side, but now he intended to kill her? The President walked toward her slowly, grinning, almost daring her to run, but Ashanti couldn't flee. Her feet were locked in place, obeying an instinct to accept whatever fate her President assigned to her. If he said that she had to die, then she would stand still and allow herself to be killed. But as Gamba approached, Ashanti wondered why he had the right to take her life when she was merely trying to defend her family. It suddenly occurred to her that if she was *defending* the hive and the President was attacking her, then *he* must be Antistan's enemy. The President continued to advance, and still Ashanti did not move. But now she had no intention of submitting—now she was prepared to fight.

President Gamba saw the subtle shift in her posture and the hard look in her eyes. He hesitated. He had expected Ashanti to run, in which case he would have laughed at her cowardice or chased her down and ripped her legs off one at a time. But she was waiting for him, and she looked far more capable than any worker he'd ever seen.

General Ainsley Walters stepped in front of Ashanti, facing President Gamba.

The Antistani President stared up at the General, surprised, but grateful to be saved from the conflict.

"Get out of my way!" he ordered.

General Walters didn't respond. Ashanti stood behind the big soldier, shocked that President Gamba had wanted to kill her, surprised that she had been ready to fight him, and hardly believing that the Alpha Zee general was had intervened.

Gamba turned to Ambassador Mallen. "Tell him to move! He has no right to interfere!"

The look on General Walters' face made Ambassador Mallen nervous. Mallen had never seen the aggressive, capable look that a soldier gets just before he enters combat; the Ambassador was terrified to be trapped in a room with a powerful and disobedient Alpha Zee soldier who had such a cold and dispassionate sheen on his face.

"Tell him to get the hell out of my way!" Gamba said again.

Ambassador Mallen backed farther into the corner. "General," he said carefully, "this really is none of your concern."

"I'm making it my concern," General Walters said. His long mandibles had serrated edges for gripping and ripping the flesh off his enemies. They were aimed at President Gamba.

"General," Ambassador Mallen said tentatively, "you should consider the implications."

General Walters never took his eyes off Gamba.

Ambassador Mallen continued: "President Kadira ordered you to come here and apologize to President Gamba for missing his installation a month ago. What do you think he's going to say when he finds out that you disobeyed his orders, *again*, and then threatened President Gamba?"

General Walters asked, "Am I threatening you, President Gamba?" He sounded relaxed, almost disinterested, but his gaze was focused, his legs were tensed, and the pointed ends of his mandibles were aimed at Gamba's head.

It was only at that moment that President Paulo Gamba realized that he had grossly misread the situation. When General Walters had stepped in front of Ashanti, Gamba had assumed that the General was merely trying to stop the fight. He hadn't considered the possibility that General Walters was actually taking Ashanti's side. President Gamba looked up at the massive general and realized that he was far too close to the razor-sharp ends of those mandibles. No one moved in the spacious Presidential chamber. The President and the Ambassador held their breath, as if the mere sound of their breathing might trigger an attack.

"No," President Gamba said softly, taking a measured step backward, "you're not threatening me."

"That's good," General Walters said calmly, "because if I *were* threatening you, I'd be in a lot of trouble when I got back home. If I *were* threatening you, I'd be charged with treason and probably executed. If I *were* threatening you, then I might as well kill you, because I'm going to get prosecuted anyway." General Walters seemed to be unraveling before their eyes.

"I think," General Walters continued, "it's a very good thing that we all agree that I am *not* threatening you."

"Yes," President Gamba said, swallowing hard. His scar was pasty white. A single tear trickled out of his milky eye and ran down his cheek. "You absolutely are *not* threatening me." He spoke in a meek whisper.

General Walters turned his head to Ambassador Mallen. "What do you think?"

Ambassador Mallen's head bobbed quickly. "Of course not! Of course not! I don't know how that word even came out of my mouth."

General Walters stepped to the side and looked back at Ashanti. "What did you say your name was?"

"Ashanti." Her face was hot. "Ashanti Lehana."

General Walters said, "I must confess that I've grown quite cynical during the last few weeks, but you give me hope. Seeing you here restores my faith that regular citizens are capable of challenging their leaders when they think it's warranted.

You make me believe that it's still possible to change the course of life on The Great Plain."

Ashanti blushed. She'd never before been complimented as an individual, and she wasn't sure how to respond.

"You came here to say something," General Walters said, "and I want to hear you say it."

President Gamba said, "You have no right—"

General Walters turned his homicidal eyes toward the Antistani President. "She has earned the right to be heard." He turned to Ashanti and said, "Go ahead."

"Well," Ashanti said slowly, not quite sure where to begin. She looked at President Gamba. "I was listening to what you said during your daily oration, and I don't think it's fair to give the Alpha Zee thirty percent of our gross output. And then, when I looked at your face, I could tell that you didn't think it was fair either."

"She's a mind reader, too!" Ambassador Mallen exclaimed.

"Look," President Gamba said. "This trade is far too complicated for you to understand."

"What are we trading for?" Ashanti said, looking up at General Walters, who nodded encouragement.

Ambassador Mallen said carefully to General Walters. "Are you sure this is how you want to spend your influence? When I talk to President Kadira, I'm *not* going to use the word *threaten*," he said quickly. "But when President Kadira finds out that you refused to apologize and then forced President Gamba to debate with a worker, he'll strip you of your rank. Are you really willing to throw away your career so that we can debate issues that Ashanti will never understand in a million years?"

"Ambassador Mallen," General Walters said, "you're, by far, the smartest ant in our colony. You're very good at figuring things out, right?"

"I like to think so," Ambassador Mallen preened.

"Then how come you haven't yet figured out that I don't care about my career?"

Ambassador Mallen had no response.

"Doesn't it amaze you," the General said, "that a mere worker, sitting in the great chamber, listening to her President's daily oration, hearing chanting citizens all around her, somehow blocked out all the noise and actually *heard* the message and understood the issue well enough to come up here and challenge it?"

Ambassador Mallen said, "I guess I'm not as easily impressed as you are. But if this is the way you want to go out, that's fine with me." He turned to Ashanti, speaking in a condescending tone. "Listen, Ashanti dear, the Alpha Zee Colony has made a very big commitment to Antistan that—"

"What kind of commitment?" she asked.

Ambassador Mallen shrugged. "We've built up your infrastructure, plus we've increased the labor pool, which increased the yield, which works in everyone's favor. All boats rise in a tide, right?"

Ashanti had no idea what a boat or a tide was, but she didn't let that distract her.

"What does infrastructure mean?" she asked.

The Ambassador smiled. He believed he was one of the few ants on The Great Plain who could really understand these complicated issues. "Infrastructure includes things like the depots, production procedures, storage facility, transportation routes, and that sort of thing."

"We had all the *infrastructure* we needed before the Alpha Zee arrived," Ashanti said. "So why should we pay the Alpha Zee to help us do what we've been doing by ourselves for years? The only reason the Alpha Zee invested in storage facilities and transportation routes is that they're taking so much of our crop that it can't all be carried out in one day. All of the investments the Alpha Zee have made here have been for their benefit, not ours. So why should we pay for them?"

President Gamba looked uncertain. The way she laid it out, the deal didn't seem quite so generous. "I think you're a little confused about what's happening here, Ashanti."

"Am I?" she said. "Everyone in the colony knows that a worker consumes about twenty-five percent of the food produced from the leaves that she gathers. The only thing you've said that I agree with is that between wars, soldiers do very little work, but what you failed to mention is that between wars, they also don't move very much. Each soldier literally stands in one spot all day, watching his assigned area. And because he doesn't move, he doesn't require much food. Although a soldier is bigger than I am, he eats far less than I do. If we have an especially good harvest, soldiers still eat only what they need, and if we have a lean period, the soldiers go on rations just like the rest of us. Can't you see how expensive it is for us to pay the Alpha Zee military to do what we could easily do for ourselves?"

"Ah," Ambassador Mallen said quickly, "that's why you're a worker, not a thinker." He winked at President Gamba. "You just don't appreciate the subtleties of this agreement. For example, you failed to mention that if you produce less, the Alpha Zee takes less in payment. But," he paused dramatically, "the Alpha Zee will not reduce your military protection during those lean times. On top of that, Alpha Zee protection is far superior to Antistani protection. We've developed such a powerful reputation that no one will even challenge us."

"So we're paying you more than we would pay our own soldiers because no one is likely to attack us while we're under your protection?" Ashanti asked.

"That's right."

"It's a deterrence strategy."

General Walters regarded Ashanti with real respect. This was an amazing ant.

"Yes, I like that," Ambassador Mallen said. "A deterrence strategy. Well put."

"How many troops do you have stationed here?"

"Oh, I don't know the exact numbers."

"More than we had when we had our own military?"

"Oh, heavens no!" Ambassador Mallen said, laughing. "This is more of an elite strike team, perfectly positioned to broadcast the Alpha Zee's presence to any attacking force and perfectly suited to handle any conflict."

"So how big a force compared to our previous military?" Ashanti pushed. "Half as much? A quarter?"

Ambassador Mallen waved her off. "Your military was bloated and inefficient. I don't think direct comparisons are instructive. What we have in place is a very capable force."

"Do you see what he's done, President Gamba?" Ashanti said. "We're giving away our valuable fungus while the actual military protection we're getting is minimal. The Alpha Zee isn't actually giving us enough soldiers to protect us. They're hoping that their reputation will be enough to deter any attack. For weeks, I have not come across a *single* Alpha Zee soldier while I've been foraging.

"Is . . . is. . . that true, Ambassador Mallen?" President Gamba asked, nervously.

"Are you going to take the unsolicited advice of a worker? Listen, she doesn't understand military strategy. She doesn't know how many troops we have, how many are needed, or where they should be positioned."

"But there *are* enough troops to protect us?" President Gamba insisted.

"You live under the Alpha Zee umbrella," Ambassador Mallen said. "You've got the best protection on The Great Plain."

"The best *deterrence* on The Great Plain," Ashanti said.

"That's what I said."

"No, it's not," Ashanti said. "We're only getting the best *deterrence*, not the best *protection*. If deterrence doesn't work, and someone attacks *your* mound, Alpha Zee soldiers will gladly give their lives to protect their Queen. But those same soldiers are not going to give their lives to protect *our* Queen. Why would they?" Ashanti turned to President Gamba. "If the Queen happens to survive the attack, then Ambassador Mallen will surely come back to you and demand even more fungus if you want his troops to provide further deterrence. We'll fall into a cycle where we pay them progressively more while they give us progressively less!"

"This . . . insubordinate . . . ant," Ambassador Mallen huffed, "doesn't know what she's talking about!"

"You're wrong about that," General Ainsley Walters said, gazing at Ashanti with more pride and respect than he'd ever felt for any ant. "She is a truly brilliant patriot. She should be given a position in the government."

Ashanti blushed and smiled at the general.

"What she should do," President Gamba growled, "is get back to *work*!" He marched past the general and shoved Ashanti out into the corridor. When he turned to come back into the room, General Walters grabbed him around the neck with his powerful pinchers.

"Ow! Ow! Ow!" Gamba squealed.

"If you *ever* touch her again," General Walters said, pausing for several seconds, glaring into Gamba's good eye. "I will kill you."

"Okay! Okay!" Gamba said. Tears rolled down his cheeks. "Please! Please!"

"*That* is a threat," General Walters said to Ambassador Mallen. "If you want to tell President Kadira that I threatened someone, tell him about my promise to kill Paulo Gamba."

"I'm not going to say *anything* to *anyone*!" Ambassador Mallen said desperately. Urine ran down his back legs.

General Walters looked back toward Ashanti, who was standing in the hallway. "You should go," he said.

Ashanti nodded and backed away, not wanting to break eye contact with General Walters. Thoughts were swirling in her head, and she didn't understand the crazy feelings gurgling in her stomach.

"Thank you," she said. She wanted to touch the General, to hug him. It was the first time in her life she'd ever felt the urge to have affectionate contact with another ant. But she turned and ran away.

When General Walters finally released President Gamba, the Antistani leader slumped to the ground, gasping for breath. Ambassador Mallen cowered in a corner, trying to make himself invisible.

General Walters looked around the room, and then calmly walked out.

Ashanti returned to work, feeling dreamy. She was angry that President Gamba had seemed so blind to the deceptions of Ambassador Mallen, but she was proud that she'd spoken to him. And she couldn't stop thinking about General Ainsley Walters and the way that he had looked at her. She was full of questions, and she was sure that General Walters could answer most of them.

Ashanti tried to clear her mind as she ferried leaf after leaf back to the mound. After hours of labor, she staggered toward the hive with her final load as a thin blade of sunlight cut through clouds on the horizon. She labored up the side of the mound, swaying from side to side. She reached the depot and released her burden into the deep pile of leaves. She turned her creaking neck from side to side and began the long commute to her home on the north side of the mound. When she finally reached her quarters, she collapsed and dreamed all night of General Ainsley Walters.

thirteen

When Ashanti Lehana awoke the next morning, she knew exactly what to do; General Walters had given her confidence a boost, and Ambassador Mallen had unwittingly provided the answer to Antistan's problems. She ran down the hallway to the central meeting room where everyone was gathered to hear the President's daily oration. She pushed through the crowd, saying hello to her friends as she made her way to her assigned spot.

"You look awfully happy," Justine Ricardo said.

"She does, doesn't she?" Laura Mejia said, observing the flush in Ashanti's face and the excitement in her eyes.

"I've got an idea," Ashanti said, grinning. "Remember yesterday we thought giving Alpha Zee thirty percent of the gross sounded like too much?"

"Yeah?"

"Well, I talked to President Gamba and told him that I thought the deal was unfair, and—"

"*You* talked to the *President?*" Justine exclaimed, her mouth gaping.

"You shouldn't have done that!" Laura shivered, as if she felt a sudden chill.

"What was he like?" Justine asked. "He looks so powerful on his platform."

"Humph," Ashanti said. "He looked tiny next to General Walters."

"General Walters?" Justine said.

"Who's that?" Laura asked.

Ashanti smiled. "He's . . ." Her eyes turned toward the ceiling searching for the right word. "He's an ally," she said dreamily.

Justine and Laura looked at each other. "An ally for what?" Justine said.

"An ally for Antistan," Ashanti said. "I've figured out how to undo the contract with Alpha Zee, but I'll need your help."

"Of course," Justine said.

Ashanti shared her plan with her friends, and though they listened attentively, they didn't get it. They stared at her with blank eyes.

"Hello?" Ashanti said. "Are you still with me?"

"Yeah," Laura scowled. "but I don't know how to do that."

"Me neither," Justine said. They both looked wrought with confusion.

"It'll be easier than you think," Ashanti said. She leaned forward and rubbed her antennae against theirs. "Pass this scent message to everyone you see and tell them to pass it to everyone that *they* see."

The workers stood still for the President's oration, but Ashanti didn't hear a word of it, and when the chanting began, she again resisted the instinct to join in. Instead she wondered if General Walters was still in Antistan or if he had returned to the Alpha Zee mound. She hoped that he wouldn't get in too much trouble for his actions yesterday, and she prayed that she would see him again.

Ashanti did not carry a single leaf that day. She moved from ant to ant in the foraging areas, sharing her scent message, and within a few hours, millions of Antistani workers were executing her plan: They slowed down production.

Yesterday, Ambassador Mallen had said that if Antistan produced less, the Alpha Zee would take less, so Ashanti calculated that a dramatic reduction in crop yields might give President Gamba the leverage he needed to renegotiate the contract.

However, slowing production went against the genetic instincts of every worker in Antistan, so Ashanti had to help them overcome those instincts. She included a powerful chant in the scent message she shared with her sisters and brothers; the ants sang it throughout the day.

"WE ARE NOT . . . ALPHA ZEE SLAVES!

"WE ARE NOT . . . ALPHA ZEE SLAVES!"

Instead of continually exhorting their sisters to move faster, work leaders reminded them to take their time.

"No sprinting!" they yelled occasionally.

"WE ARE NOT . . . ALPHA ZEE SLAVES!" the workers responded, reducing their pace.

Ashanti had always enjoyed standing over the collection warehouses, seeing the deep pile of leaves the workers had amassed, but she now delighted in the relatively small daily payload as the citizens of Antistan began a work slowdown that would stretch on for months.

fourteen

"What can I do?" President Gamba smirked. He'd just left the Senate chambers where the latest production report revealed that fungus outputs had decreased again, falling to nearly half the normal level. "The workers just aren't bringing in leaves as quickly as they used to."

"That's not the Alpha Zee's problem," Ambassador Mallen said. He stretched a leg behind him and scrunched his face, trying, without success, to scratch his back.

"Actually, it is," Gamba said. "You're getting your thirty percent, but it's not as much as it used to be."

Ambassador Mallen shook his head. "We have to take the quantity that we need regardless of the production rates." He tried another leg, stretching it up his corpulent flank, rubbing back and forth.

"If you do that," President Gamba warned, "some of the workers will starve."

"Since when do you care about the workers?" The Ambassador leaned against the wall and shifted back and forth with half-lidded eyes. Finally, he scratched the right spot and sighed contentedly.

"I don't," Gamba shrugged, "but if they die that's even fewer ants to produce fungus."

"Believe me," Ambassador Mallen said, "as soon as a few of them starve to death, the rest will end this silly slowdown."

"Maybe."

"We're suffering an unacceptable shortage on our end," Mallen said. "Our citizens have come to rely on their fungus, and during the past few moons, our reserves have dwindled." Alpha Zee had stored up a three-month supply, and already more than half of that had been consumed in order to supplement the relatively small daily shipments from Antistan.

"So your citizens will have to get used to a little less," President Gamba said. "You said yourself that it will only take the death of a few workers to break this effort."

"Yes," Mallen agreed, "but are you so politically naïve that you expect my President to sit back and do nothing while Antistani workers choke off Alpha Zee's lawful resource? Do you expect Present Kadira to stand in front of his constituents and tell them that they're not going to receive the fungus that they love—and *need*—so much? Surely, you don't think that he'll take political heat just because you've proven to be such an abject failure at controlling your own colony."

"You took away my military!" General Gamba cried. "How do you expect me to control them?"

"You still have an internal force."

"It's not enough to marshal all of the citizens."

"Then you'll have to manipulate them the same way my President does," Ambassador Mallen said. "You have to use persuasion."

"Persuasion doesn't work," President Gamba scoffed.

Ambassador Mallen shook his head slowly. "Sometimes I think we made an error in judgment when we chose you to lead Antistan." President Gamba bristled at this insult and looked, for a moment, as if he might attack the Ambassador. If Mallen noticed the danger, he showed no sign. "Persuasion works far more effectively than force, because the citizens come to believe as you believe. Persuasion, when used correctly, can enslave without resistance."

President Gamba shuffled his feet and looked at Ambassador Mallen doubtfully.

"Are you aware," the Ambassador continued, "that our military never operates within our own mound?"

President Gamba asked, "Never?"

"Never," Ambassador Mallen said. "The citizens of the Alpha Zee are free. Free to move. Free to think. Free to act. Every day, my President gets up and delivers an oration to these free ants and compels them to freely adopt his beliefs. You know why it works? Because he is *persuasive*. That's what you need to learn—how to persuade. In the meantime, your agreement with us is changing. Instead of a strict percentage of the crop, we'll take thirty percent of the gross *or* twelve cryons daily, whichever is greater."

"*Twelve* cryons!" President Gamba exclaimed. "Half our population will die."

"Well," Ambassador Mallen said with a shrug so vicious that Gamba shuddered. "You'd better persuade them to work harder."

Gamba stared off into the distance.

"You know what you could do in the meantime?" Ambassador Mallen asked, as if the idea had just occurred to him. "You could supplement their diets with something that tastes even better than fungus."

fifteen

"These are tough times," President Paulo Gamba boomed from his high perch, "but it's during the toughest times that our strengths are revealed." Antistani citizens looked up with eager, expectant faces. "We've improved our efficiency!" Gamba lied. "We've collected more leaves! But our population is so much bigger now that there's not enough fungus to serve everyone. So I've arranged for emergency rations that will arrive this evening."

"The Alpha Zee is bringing back some of our fungus?" someone in the crowd asked with a voice filled with real hope.

"Better than that," President Gamba beamed. "They're going to deliver *honeydew.*"

No one in the crowd knew what to make of that. Did this mean that the Alpha Zee hive was responding to their production slowdown?

That evening, a long convoy of Alpha Zee honeypot repletes marched into Antistan. They looked like queens ready to give birth, but instead of abdomens full of eggs, the ants carried enough amber fluid to feed millions. They set up feeding stations throughout Antistan. Each position was marked with a *Golden H* formed by crystallized honeydew. The Alpha Zee maintained enormous aphid herds, but until now, the tribe had never found an external market for the cheap, quick honeydew the aphids produced.

"Help yourselves!" President Gamba exclaimed. "Get as much as you like!"

Lines formed in front of the repletes, who produced droplets of amber liquid between their mandibles. The citizens of Antistan stepped forward to gulp it down.

"It's so sweet!" Justine exclaimed.

"Yes it is," Ashanti agreed, gobbling at a rate that embarrassed her. She hated to think that President Gamba was using their hunger to manipulate them, but she couldn't deny that the honeydew soothed her parched throat in a way she'd never imagined possible.

"You're a hero," Ambassador Mallen said when Gamba returned to the Presidential chamber.

President Gamba's milky eye seemed to smile. "Yes, I suppose I am."

"Honeydew is a quick and easy meal," Ambassador Mallen said. "And we can definitely take care of the needs of all your citizens."

"The way I understand it," President Gamba said, "you've actually got too much honeydew. You've allowed your aphid herds to grow so large that they're producing more honeydew than ten trillion ants could eat."

Ambassador Mallen's face darkened. "That's not true."

"But you've gotta admit it's pretty damned plentiful," President Gamba said.

"Not in Antistan," Ambassador Mallen pointed out.

"True," President Gamba said. "But we've got fungus."

"Have you taken a look at your citizens lately?" Ambassador Mallen asked. "If they're going to continue this slowdown, which they shouldn't, but if they are, then you've got to get food in them. You can't just let them die."

"I'm willing to negotiate," President Gamba said.

"Good," Mallen said. "We'll set up *Golden H* feeding stations throughout your hive and provide meals for your entire population every day."

President Gamba stroked his mandibles. "We don't need honeydew every day. Maybe just once or twice a week."

"You'll get a better deal on daily delivery," Mallen said, as if the honeydew would be ferried in every morning rather than produced on site by a herd of aphids that the Alpha Zee would relocate to Antistan. "We'll trade you honeydew for fungus. It's really a perfect match. Your workers are good at producing fungus, and the Alpha Zee is good at delivering honeydew."

"But we don't *need* honeydew," Gamba insisted.

"Why not let the citizens decide?" Mallen said. "If they like it, they'll eat a lot of it. If they don't, they won't. You'll pay only for what they consume." It was a safe bet for Ambassador Mallen, because he knew that once he set up enough *Golden H* feeding locations to make honeydew a convenient and effortless meal, Antistani citizens would quickly become addicted. Although honeydew was nutritionally deficient, it had an irresistible flavor.

"I only pay for what they eat?" Gamba asked, believing he was negotiating shrewdly.

"Only what they eat," Mallen promised.

"What's the exchange rate?"

"On daily delivery we can give you two-to-one."

President Gamba laughed. He wasn't an expert at trade agreements, but he knew that the fungus that his colony produced was at least ten times more valuable than honeydew. *Two-to-one, indeed.* If Antistan was going to purchase honeydew in volume, he should get a rate of fifteen-to-one or even twenty-to-one.

"Two-to-one is pretty good," Ambassador Mallen smiled.

President Gamba smiled back at the obese little ant. "Do you think I'm a fool?"

Ambassador Mallen shrugged. "Those are the terms."

"I'll shop around," President Gamba said. "I hear Anterbijan has a pretty healthy honeydew operation."

"So we're back to threats?" Ambassador Mallen asked. "I shouldn't have to say this to you, President Gamba, but I will: If you sell your fungus to another colony, you will no longer be President of Antistan."

Gamba glared at the Ambassador. "I thought the Alpha Zee believed in free trade."

"We do. We also believe in commitments. We gave you the presidency that you wanted, so you're obligated to give us the fungus that we want."

"But your terms are terrible."

"You're forgetting about our military support," Ambassador Mallen said. "That's worth something."

"You can't keep using that as an excuse to take whatever you want from us," President Gamba said.

"If you prefer, we could pull our troops out, keep our honeydew at home, and leave you to deal with foreign armies."

Gamba sighed and stared into the distance. That option would have been attractive if he possessed any semblance of a regular army. But if the Alpha Zee military left, his colony would immediately fall under attack by rivals.

"We'll leave if you want us to," Ambassador Mallen offered again.

"You know I can't let you leave," President Gamba said.

"Then what are we haggling about?"

Suddenly a loud boom reverberated through the hive.

"What the hell was—" General Gamba asked. Before he could complete the question, two more explosions rocked the chamber. Gamba and Mallen stepped out into the hallway. Workers and caretakers were running wildly in every direction. The scent of panic flooded the crowded corridors.

"What happened?" President Gamba demanded.

"In the feeding area," a worker responded without slowing down. "A replete exploded."

"Exploded?" Mallen asked. That didn't seem possible.

The President and the Ambassador slowly made their way down to the cafeteria where the repletes had been stationed. The scene was absolute mayhem. Honeydew was splattered all over the walls, and the floor was littered with the bodies of hundreds of dead and dying Antistani citizens.

"What's that smell?" Mallen asked. An acrid odor hung in the air. It was unlike anything that Mallen had ever smelled.

President Gamba's antennae sampled the pheromone carefully. "I don't know."

"*Camponotus*," General Ainsley Walters said, standing behind them.

"What are *you* doing here?" Mallen asked, nervously. He was terrified of the big general.

"I was with a platoon just outside the mound. We came in as soon as we heard the explosions."

"What's a *Camponotus*?" Mallen asked.

"It's a type of parasitic ant," General Walters said. "They can mask their scent and live among you for years, and if they ever feel under threat of detection, they have glands along their flanks filled with toxic chemicals. They compress their abdomens in a particular way and explode, spraying deadly chemicals in every direction. We've encountered them in other hives."

"One of them was here?"

"Probably a lot of them are here."

"Why are they here?" Mallen asked.

"They're living in an environment that is hospitable for them," General Walters said. "You've disbanded the Antistani military, so any parasite looking for a home can relocate here without fear."

"The *Alpha Zee* military is supposed to protect us!" President Gamba exclaimed, his scar turning beet red.

"Oh, don't worry. We'll keep rival *armies* from attacking you," General Walters said placidly, "but we can't do much about parasites and terrorists."

"What do you mean *terrorists?*" President Gamba asked.

General Walters turned to Ambassador Mallen and said, "You want to tell him about the wasps?"

President Gamba already knew about Yasura Hasan, the wasp who had caused the pseudo civil war in Antistan, but he didn't know about the eggs that she'd laid on the caterpillar cocoons in the mound.

Lucas Mallen, despite his great intellect, hadn't considered the long-term implication of those eggs.

"I did my research," Mallen said defensively. "When a wasp lays her eggs inside of an ant mound, only about ten percent of them usually survive. That seemed like an acceptable risk to accomplish our goals."

"Yes, ten percent—*if* Antistan had a military," General Walters corrected. "Adult wasps have the ability to chemically confuse the ants, but the juvenile wasps aren't as talented. If Antistan had a military, the soldiers would have detected and killed ninety percent of the wasp larvae immediately after they hatched. The remaining ten percent would have barely escaped with their lives. But since you got rid of the military, no one took on the task of detecting and killing the juvenile wasps. And since the wasps were not under threat, they had no reason to leave. They're all still here emitting, a scent that identifies them as full-blooded Antistani citizens."

"Wait a second. You're saying that there are wasps in the hive now?" President Gamba asked, nervously. He was speaking to General Walters, but he was glaring at Ambassador Mallen with his good eye.

"I'm certain that they're here," General Walters said. "And I'm sure that the terrorists and the parasites are all pissed off about the meager food rations here."

"So they're terrorizing to get more food?" Ambassador Mallen wondered.

"Mostly they terrorize because they're angry," General Walters said. "They're not smart enough to know exactly who or what is causing their food shortage, so they lash out at anyone."

"What are we going to do about that?" President Gamba demanded.

General Walters chuckled. "*We?*" He turned and left the cafeteria, still laughing.

sixteen

It was a bright, clear day on The Great Plain, with barely a whisper of wind tickling the petals of the flowers. Herds of buffalo, impalas, zebras, and wildebeests grazed languidly in the shimmering distance, relaxed in the knowledge that most predators would sleep through the hottest part of the day.

Everyone seemed calm except Ambassador Lucas Mallen. He had a death grip on the winged soldier who was ferrying him back to the Alpha Zee mound.

"Can we stop for a minute?" Ambassador Mallen screamed into the soldier's ear. The Ambassador's face was contorted in terror and his eyes were wet with tears.

"We're just about there," the soldier replied. He flew in a straight line with little of the jinxing and diving that other insects performed to avoid birds of prey. Birds knew better than to attack an Alpha Zee flyer. Now that the soldiers were dining almost exclusively on fungus, they could fly the entire eighty-coron distance between Antistan and Alpha Zee in just over three hours.

"But I'm . . . I'm . . . slipping!" Ambassador Mallen's tiny limbs were not quite up to the task of holding his bulky frame in place.

The soldier sighed and descended, almost losing the Ambassador as he banked to the ground. He landed softly among towering blades of grass just ten corons from Alpha Zee.

Ambassador Mallen scrambled down and stretched his legs and neck.

"Whew!" he said. "I guess I'm getting old." He flexed his forelegs. "I was a lot stronger when I was younger."

The soldier looked doubtful. "We're going to be late, sir. You're expected in the Senate in just a few minutes." Although Lucas Mallen bore the Pheromone of Honor and was well-respected within the Alpha Zee hive, he was not popular among the soldiers. Thanks to Mallen, the focus and scope of the military's mission had changed. Most of the troops spent their days patrolling the expansive perimeter of The Grove, living solitary and dangerous lives far away from their extended family, and far away from the Queen, who inspired their dedication. Their mortality rate was nearly 40 percent compared to just 4 percent for soldiers who lived in and around the Alpha Zee hive. They knew that Lucas Mallen, the corpulent ant living a pampered life as an ambassador, was the architect of their current military deployments, and they resented him for it.

"Surely you planned rest stops," Ambassador Mallen lectured. "Civilians aren't used to hanging onto soldiers in flight; we need a break every now and again."

"Sir, I've carried many civilians. You're the first one who needed a break."

"Well!" Ambassador Mallen sniffed, staring off into the grass.

"I could carry you in my mandibles," the soldier offered.

To Ambassador Mallen's shame, the offer was enticing, but he had too much pride to return to the Alpha Zee mound ferried like a helpless pupal ant.

"Absolutely not!" he exclaimed indignantly.

The soldier shrugged.

"Okay," Ambassador Mallen said after a few minutes. He climbed back on board. "But not too fast!"

Soon the Alpha Zee hive appeared in the distance. The sight of it always made Ambassador Mallen gasp in amazement. The dark soil of the hive was so rich that it glistened in the sunlight. A squadron from the Alpha Zee air force patrolled the airspace around the mound. Several winged fighters approached and scanned Ambassador Mallen suspiciously before allowing his transport to continue.

Finally, the soldier landed, and Ambassador Mallen tumbled off awkwardly, landing flat on his back with his legs flailing in the air. He tried to hook a foot in the dirt to flip over, but his body was too rotund and his legs too short. He couldn't get any leverage. His face turned red and his breath grew labored as he rolled back and forth. After a few moments, he stopped flopping and stared up at the soldier.

"Would you mind?" Ambassador Mallen said quietly.

"Would I mind what?" the soldier said with a straight face.

"Helping me?"

"Helping you with what, sir?"

Ambassador Mallen glowered at him. "Helping me stand up!"

The soldier plucked Ambassador Mallen off the ground effortlessly. The Ambassador dusted himself off and stood as tall as he could.

"You should be more respectful!" he admonished.

"I'm sorry, sir. I didn't realize that you were stuck."

"I'm not as young as I used to be," Ambassador Mallen said defensively.

"No, sir."

The Ambassador marched into the mound and issued a slow, delighted sigh. Every time he came home, he realized how much he missed the simple pleasures. The Alpha Zee Colony had wide, clean corridors, a ventilation system that kept the air at a moderate temperature year-round, a plumbing network, a waste removal system, ornate public structures and assembly halls, and large, lavishly appointed living quarters. Everywhere Ambassador Mallen looked, he saw happy, well-fed citizens. The colony had several cafeterias, where an ant could get anything from protein to sugars to vegetables to drinks.

The Ambassador made his way to the heavily guarded Senate chamber deep within the mound. The leaders gathered daily to decide whether the colony should expand its physical structure, change its larvae-care procedures, develop new food gathering strategies, revise immigration rules, and most importantly, adjust the Queen's birthing patterns.

"We need more soldiers," Senator James Lucasson said just as Ambassador Mallen entered the room.

"The only way we can protect our interests is with an adequate military." He stood at the front of the room, debating with Senator Thomas Marshall while the other members of the Senate listened attentively.

"We have more than enough soldiers," countered Senator Marshall, who was a special hybrid that the Queen had created. As Alpha Zee had adopted more species from other hives, Queen Wenonah had mated with many of the new fertile males, believing that their sperm would allow her to mix and match the traits of different species to develop ants with an extraordinary range of talents. She had designed hybrids to form an internal police force and to become members of the Senate. Hybrids had the bulky frames of soldiers, the diligence of workers, the patience of caretakers, unprecedented intelligence, and a calm disposition that allowed them to apply non-lethal solutions to conflicts among Alpha Zee residents.

"What we need," Senator Marshall said, "are more workers, harvesters and caretakers. We should make the mound a better place to live, rather than always trying to conquer new territory."

"Our fighting forces are wasting away!" Senator Lucasson said. "Every day we tell the Queen to produce a smaller number of soldiers. And every day we grow weaker while our enemies grow stronger."

"You're exaggerating," Senator Marshall said. "Yes, our fighting forces are smaller than they were six months ago, but we're still bigger than the next ten armies *combined*. We're still committing 25 percent of our eggs to the military, plus we control all of the fungus production in The Grove, so we have sufficient energy to easily overrun ninety-five percent of the colonies on The Great Plain. Against each of the remaining five percent, we have, at worst, a seven-to-one advantage in fighting forces. None of them would dare attack us."

"Your naïveté," Senator Lucasson sneered, "is breathtaking. We're vulnerable in ways that a pacifist like you just wouldn't understand?"

"Really? Where is our vulnerability?"

"The Great Plain is changing," Senator Lucasson hissed. "The debate is no longer about armies and colonies. It's about disaffected groups. It's about wasps who infiltrate using chemical and biological weapons. Are you so blind that you can't see that we have to defend ourselves against an entirely new type of threat?"

"A wasp?" Senator Marshall laughed. "Here?"

"How do you know that we don't have parasites living among us as we speak?" Senator Lucasson challenged. "Luckily, Ambassador Mallen had the wisdom to institute the parasite sweeping procedures for the Queen, which uncovered the spies nesting on her body. But parasites mimicking our scent could be walking through our tunnels, eating our food and doing whatever they wanted for days, weeks or months, waiting for the right moment to strike."

"If that's true," Senator Marshall said, "then what good will more soldiers do us? If these hidden parasites exist, *new* soldiers won't be able to detect them any better than our current soldiers. And if the parasites reveal themselves, we have more than enough military force to neutralize them."

"All right, Senators," interrupted President Kadira. "We need to postpone this discussion because Ambassador Mallen has returned from Antistan with a report. Ambassador, what do you have for us?"

Ambassador Mallen shuffled to the front of the room. "Unfortunately," he began, "the situation in Antistan is not improving. The *Camponotus* are blowing themselves up left and right, killing hundreds of innocent civilians at a time. We suspect that there might be two or three generations of wasps operating in and around the hive, and the workers have continued their slowdown despite losing nearly ten percent of their population to starvation."

"How long do you think the slowdown will continue?" the President asked, ignoring the issue of wasps and suicide bombers and focusing on fungus production.

Ambassador Mallen shook his head in a gesture that suggested the futility of trying to predict what the citizens of Antistan would do. "A worker named Ashanti Lehana has organized them, and they seem pretty committed to her. Every day, they wake up, carry out their dead, and return with fewer leaves. They seem to rejoice in the small loads, and they're always chanting that they won't be Alpha Zee slaves."

"That's outrageous!" President Kadira exclaimed. "She's brainwashed them into believing that they'll be slaves if they honor a trade agreement?"

"Those infidels—"

"—have no—"

"—work ethic!" the Secretaries spat.

"They'd rather—"

"—starve than do—"

"—an honest day's work!"

"What can we do about it?" Senator Lucasson asked.

Ambassador Mallen said, "We're exporting honeydew to them, but it's only helping a little bit. Since their production is so low, most of the ants aren't getting *any* fungus, so they rely on honeydew for *all* of their meals, and they're developing health problems."

Ambassador Mallen mentioned these health issues only in passing, and no one in the chamber asked for elaboration. They all knew that only two or three species of ants could eat honeydew for every meal. For anyone else, eating too often at the *Golden H* locations, led to weakness, bloating, and, eventually, death.

"I've told Gamba that he has to compel his workers to pick up the pace," Mallen said, "but he claims he can't do anything because he has no military."

"So let's send some troops down there to quiet things down," Senator Lucasson said, quickly. "Our soldiers can get the workers to do their jobs again, and cure the insurgency."

"We've already got soldiers patrolling the area," Ambassador Mallen said.

"Are the soldiers actually *inside* Antistan?" Senator Lucasson asked.

"No," the Ambassador conceded.

"Well, that's the problem. Get our troops inside where they can do some good."

"Done!" President Kadira said. "We'll send twenty-five thousand soldiers down tomorrow."

"But somehow, we have to deal with Ashanti Lehana," Ambassador Mallen said.

"Can we kill her?" Senator Lucasson asked.

"Not without turning her into a martyr," Ambassador Mallen lied. He was desperate to keep Ashanti safe, because he feared General Walter's reaction if anything happened to her. "Given the loyalty the workers have toward her, it would only make the situation worse."

"Come now," President Kadira said, "surely that can't be true. Citizens of every colony have notoriously short memories. If we removed Ashanti Lehana, they'd forget about her in a matter of weeks."

"These ants are different," Mallen lied again. "You see that they've initiated an unprecedented work slowdown, so I'm convinced that if we allow Ashanti to become a cause celebre, it will only strengthen their resolve."

"How much of a militant is she?" Senator Lucasson asked.

"A few weeks ago, she burst into the President's private quarters and threatened him," Mallen said.

"Are you *serious*?" President Kadira asked.

"I was there."

"You hear that, Marshall, you damned pacifist?" Senator Lucasson said staring hard at his Senate rival. "We've let things get so lax in Antistan that a *worker* has challenged the President."

Senator Marshall waved dismissively.

Ambassador Mallen said, "Then she engaged in open warfare against the Alpha Zee by organizing this worker slowdown. We also believe that she has destroyed leaves when her sisters delivered more than she wanted them to deliver."

"She's a terrorist!" Senator Lucasson said.

Mallen shrugged noncommittally.

"Do we have any idea where the terrorists are located in the mound?" President Kadira asked.

"They could be anywhere," Mallen said.

"I bet they hang out near the medicinal plants," President Kadira said quixotically. "You know, these terrorists are going to do whatever they can to protect themselves, so if food reserves are low, don't you think they'd hang out and eat the plants the hive has gathered for medicinal purposes?"

Mallen scowled. He didn't understand the logic behind this assertion. It didn't seem obvious to him that the wasps would hang out in the medicinal chamber, but the President seemed convinced of it, so he must have access to information that was unavailable to Mallen.

In truth, the President and the Secretaries had formulated a plan of their own that was designed to end the work slowdown in Antistan. If they destroyed the colony's store of medicinal plants, then the risk of disease would increase dramatically.

"They wouldn't dare—"

"—continue to starve themselves—"

"—if they've also lost their medicine," the Secretaries said.

"That would be suicide," President Kadira agreed. "Bodies weakened by a lack of food cannot also fight off diseases, so if they lose their medicine, they'll have to get back to work in order to strengthen themselves."

President Kadira strode onto his platform high in the main chamber of Alpha Zee. He waved at his citizens and they waved back enthusiastically.

"We are peace lovers!" he began, the jowls of his tanned face shaking.

"PEACE LOVERS!" the audience roared back.

"We are freedom lovers!" President Kadira said, following the script he used to begin and end every oration.

"FREEDOM LOVERS!" the crowd agreed.

"Those who attack our freedom must be exterminated!" He raised a fist and slammed it into his open palm.

"EXTERMINATED!" the crowd said, driving their fists into their palms.

"Their networks must be destroyed!"

"DESTROYED!"

"Every colony on The Great Plain must stand up and be counted!" President Kadira said. "They are either with us, or they are against us."

"WITH US OR AGAINST US!"

"Any colony that does not stand *with* us is the enemy!"

"THE ENEMY!"

"And they will suffer the consequences!"

"THEY WILL SUFFER!"

"Because we are peace lovers!"

"PEACE LOVERS!"

"We are freedom lovers!"

"FREEDOM LOVERS!"

"Citizens of Alpha Zee, I come to you today with grave news," the President said. "Some of you have undoubtedly noticed that our daily shipments of fungus have been reduced. First, I want to commend you for your selflessness in the face of this crisis, and I want to assure you that we are doing everything we can to rectify the situation."

He paused to let this praise sink in. His citizens loved to be told how noble they were, and how much they'd sacrificed for the greater good. Although Alpha Zee contained every imaginable amenity and the residents consumed more resources than any other colony on The Great Plain, its citizens loved the notion that they were moderate, self-sacrificing ants who lived on meager rations.

"The problem," President Kadira continued, "stems from terrorist cells in Antistan. They've blown up *Golden H* providers, stolen leaves, chemically destroyed huge chambers stuffed with fungus—and all with the goal of cutting off our food supply."

The crowd booed.

"Not only that … we also believe that there may be terrorists among us," President Kadira said ominously.

The crowd gasped.

"So stay alert for anything unusual. If you detect a parasite or an ant that you believe is a terrorist, tell someone in law enforcement immediately."

Every antenna in the room started sweeping back and forth frantically sampling the pheromones in the air, looking for infiltrators. But it was a futile effort. If terrorists existed in the mound, they would have expertly mimicked the pheromones of Alpha Zee citizens, so no one would detect them. The President's warning made the citizens anxious, suspicious and easier to manipulate, but it did nothing to improve security.

"We've learned the location of one of the primary terrorist training facilities," President Kadira said. "Within hours, a squadron of Alpha Zee fighters will make a surgical strike and destroy that target."

The crowd cheered. Alpha Zee citizens loved surgical strikes.

"We are now at war against terrorism!" the President proclaimed. "Those who maintain these terrorist networks should consider themselves forewarned. We will have zero tolerance."

"ZERO TOLERANCE!"

"After the evildoers have been rooted out," President Kadira continued, "fungus production will return to normal

levels, and we will have won another victory over the scourge
of terrorism, because we are freedom lovers!"

"FREEDOM LOVERS!"

"We are peace lovers!"

"PEACE LOVERS!"

"And those who attack freedom must be destroyed!"

"DESTROYED!"

President Kadira retreated from the platform and marched
into his private quarters, where the Secretaries stood waiting
along with General Ainsley Walters.

"That was—"

"—absolutely—"

"—brilliant!" the Secretaries of State, Defense and Homeland Security gushed.

"Mr. President," General Walters said, "with all due
respect—"

"Did I give you permission to speak?" the President interrupted.

"You should—" the Secretaries glared,

"—keep your mouth shut—"

"—until spoken to!"

The President paced back and forth in front of the General, eyeing him suspiciously. "You disobeyed a direct order."

"Yes, sir. I did." General Walters had wondered how long
it would take the little Ambassador to squeal on him.

"You were supposed to apologize to President Gamba, but
you didn't."

General Walters shook his head. "No, sir. I did not."

"You insulted him."

Insulted? Not threatened? Not assaulted? Maybe the
Ambassador hadn't told the President *everything* that had happened in Gamba's chamber.

President Kadira continued. "I had to work hard to smooth that over. Do you have any idea how difficult it is to keep this agreement in place and make sure that we receive the fungus that we need in order for our colony to function properly?"

"No, sir, I guess I don't."

"It's damned hard," the President said with a weary smile. "That's why I have to trust that when I give an order, it will be followed. You really threw me for a loop."

The President's three minions glowered at the General.

"But I'm going to give you another chance." President Kadira waited for the General to respond, but Walters said nothing. "Aren't you going to thank me?" the President asked.

"For what, sir?"

"For giving you a chance to prove your loyalty to this colony."

"I didn't know that my loyalty was in doubt."

The President studied him carefully. "Given your disobedience, it was bound to be questioned, don't you think?"

"My loyalty to our colony doesn't compel me to brutalize other colonies, sir."

"*Brutalize?*" the President laughed. "Where did that ridiculous word come from? We don't brutalize anyone. We make trade agreements, mutual-defense treaties and military-reduction pacts. We work hard to make The Grove a safer place to live—and taking out this terrorist training facility in Antistan will help us get closer to that goal."

General Walters had heard about this mission, and he wanted no part of it. "It's not a terrorist site," he said slowly. "It's a medical facility."

"What did you say?" the President stormed. He stepped into Walter's face and pressed his mandibles against the General's, almost daring the General to react.

"It's a medical facility," General Walters said evenly.

"Are you challenging me, again?" The President stormed. "I'm merely stating a well-known fact."

"Well known by whom?"

"I've seen this chamber with my own eyes," General Walters said. "It's an innocuous medical storage facility."

"Our intelligence sources say otherwise!" President Kadira asserted.

"It's definitely— "

"—a terrorist—"

"—site!" the Secretaries said.

"And we need to make these terrorists understand that we're serious," President Kadira said.

"Mr. President," General Walters said. "The citizens of Antistan are just like us. They live in close contact with each other, and maintain regurgitated food practices, so they're every bit as susceptible to disease as we are. They're fastidious about their hygiene, water safety, food storage and waste removal, and they rely on a daily ration of medicinal plants to prevent disease. If we hit this facility, we'll destroy those medicinal plants, and we'll do irreparable harm to hundreds of thousands of innocent civilians."

"It's *disguised* as a—"

"—medical facility, but it's—"

"—actually a terrorist stronghold," the Secretaries said.

"That's right," the President said. "The terrorists are tricky that way."

General Walters looked around the room, wondering what he could say to convince them that they were wrong.

"General," the President said, "what you have to understand is that we are under attack. This group of terrorists hopes to cripple us. Without fungus, we'll be forced to migrate again. They'll take control of The Grove."

General Walters was stunned by this line of reasoning. He'd never heard anything that had led him to believe that the *Camponotus* terrorists had an interest in controlling all of The Grove.

"I will not allow that to happen," the President said. "The Queen is comfortable and safe here, our workers are used to this lifestyle, and millions of ants and other creatures rely on us to protect them."

General Walters shook his head, but before he could speak, the President continued.

"I can't believe that a seasoned veteran like you needs a pep talk." President Kadira released a slow breath. "The terrorists are led by a worker named Ashanti Lehana.

General Walters' eyes widened. He hadn't seen Ashanti since the day he'd defended her from President Gamba. He was glad to hear that she was still alive, but how could the Alpha Zee government believe that she was a terrorist?

"If you know who she is, why not go after her individually?" General Walters suggested. If they gave him that mission, he'd take it. He'd track down Ashanti and help her escape from Antistan. "Why take out an entire medical center and put so many civilians at risk?"

"These things are complicated," the President said. "These terrorists don't sit in one place. We have to figure out where they train, where they store their weapons, and where they keep their information—and then hit those sites." The President paused and stroked his mandibles. "I want *you* to lead the mission."

General Walters knew that this was the reason the President had called him here. Snubbing Paulo Gamba was only a technical violation for a soldier of Walters' rank. If President Kadira really wanted to punish the General, he needed something bigger—something like disobeying a *direct* Presidential order.

"I won't do it," General Walters said, as he knew the President expected him to say.

President Kadira studied the General.

"I'm giving you an order as your commander-in-chief," President Kadira said. Now he was speaking for the record. "Are you refusing to obey that order?"

"And face court marshal—"

"—where you'll get convicted—"

"—and executed?" the Secretaries said.

"Permission to speak freely, sir?" General Walters said.

"Permission to speak freely?" the President repeated, rolling it over in his mouth. "As if you've been anything other than insubordinate up to this point?" He took a step back and studied the General. "Permission to speak freely? Hmm, now there's an interesting request. I wonder what you could possibly want to say, and whether I want to hear it. Chances are it's not worth my time."

"Definitely not—"

"—worth—"

"—your time."

President Kadira smiled and spread his forelegs in a helpless shrug. "You probably want to speak freely so that you can tell me some sad, but poignant, lesson you've learned out there on the mean old battlefields, and you think that if you deliver the story with just enough emotion and just enough regret, you might bring me to my senses. You might compel me to become a pacifist like you. Is that what you think? That speaking freely will produce some sort of epiphany? That I'll say, 'Oh my goodness, how could I have been so blind? Peace, not war! You're *right*, General. You are *so* right!' Is that what you expect, General Walters?"

General Walters regarded the President with bland patience. "No, sir."

"It's not, huh?" The President smiled. "Well, before you can speak freely, you have to tell me what you hope to accomplish. How about that? What's the goal of this conversation?"

"My own understanding, sir."

"Your own understanding? Oh, I see. Why we adopted this policy or that policy. Why the Senate approved a particular military action. Well, those are good questions, General, but you know the constraints of hive security. I can't answer questions that are above your security clearance. And even if I could, you probably wouldn't understand. It's a complicated world. We have to make decisions that have long-term ramifications, and it might not make sense to an individual ant fighting a single battle with limited information. He might not understand how he fits into the big picture, so he might get confused and have a lot of questions bubbling in his head that compel him to ask the President for permission to speak freely so that he can try to understand the big picture. Is that what we're talking about here? You want to ask questions about your military missions?"

"No, sir."

"No, sir?" the President said. "So you say you want to speak freely, but it's not to give me a lecture about morality, and it's not to question the orders that you've received over the years. Well, now you've got me all intrigued, wondering just what's rolling around in that big square head of yours. What is this question that's burning such a big hole in your mind that you have to get it out right here and right now? I suppose that, yes, you can speak freely, because now *I'm curious!*"

General Walters studied the President for a moment, then asked, "What's the definition of *free* trade?"

The President paused.

"You don't have to—"

"—answer a—"

"—traitor's questions!" the Secretaries said.

"General," the President said, "at your age and with your life experience, if you don't know what free trade is, then I don't think I can—"

"I know what *coerced* trade is," General Walters interrupted, "and what *compelled* trade is, and what *commandeered* trade is, and what *extorted* trade is, and even what *slave* trade is, but I'm just not sure what *free* trade is. And I don't see how our agreement with Antistan could possibly be called *free* trade when we enlisted a *wasp* to help us install a corrupt dictator, who disbanded the military and gave away his colony's most precious resource. Somehow we call it *free* trade when the citizens of Antistan suffer great hardship, malnutrition, and even death while we grow fat on their work product. We've turned their hive into a terrorist breeding ground, and now, you want me to make their lives even more miserable by bombing one of their medical facilities so that I can ensure that *free* trade is protected. Before I accept a mission like that, I need to know what *free* trade is."

President Kadira stepped close to General Walters. "It's hard to believe you were born with the genes of a soldier. You sound like a little crybaby caretaker."

"Waaaa!" the Secretary of State mocked, rubbing his eyes as if tears were streaming down his face.

"Wook at da wittle cwy baby!" the Secretary of Defense said.

"Him wants to know what fwee twade is, 'cause him's confwused," the Secretary of Homeland Security said.

"Walters," the President glared, "I really do wonder about your loyalty to this colony."

"He sounds—"

"—like a—"

"—traitor!" the Secretaries said.

"Guards!" the President called, smiling wickedly at General Walters. "Take him to his quarters."

"On what charge?" General Walters asked.

"Insubordination," the President snarled.

"At trial I'll argue that you gave me an unlawful order. It's my moral and ethical duty to refuse that order."

"A trial?" the President repeated laughing.

"He expects—"

"—to have—"

"—a trial!" the Secretaries exclaimed.

"I am the chief executive officer of this colony. It's well within my authority to hold you indefinitely *without* a trial, because we are in a state of war."

"War—"

"—against—"

"—terrorism!" the Secretaries repeated.

"And as long as we're at war," the President continued, "you'll be locked up."

Later that day, a squadron of winged Alpha Zee fighters used rocks dipped in formic acid to destroy a site on the northeast side Antistan.

The citizens of Alpha Zee celebrated the news during the President's daily oration.

"We hit an important terrorist training facility," the President said.

"WE HIT 'EM HARD!" the citizens screamed.

"We gave notice that we have zero tolerance for terrorism."
"ZERO TOLERANCE!"
"Those who threaten freedom will be destroyed!"
"DESTROYED!"

A week later, a team of Alpha Zee investigators discovered that the site had indeed been nothing more than a medical storage site—home to more than 50 percent of the medicine the colony would need to survive the dry season. Given the timing of the bombing, it would be impossible for Antistan to collect new reserves. The trees and bushes that produced the medicine had long since gone into hibernation. Experts predicted that disease would kill up to 20 percent of Antistan's population in the next few months.

Alpha Zee President Alexander Kadira churned with nervous energy as he took the stage a day after the report was released. Since Queen Wenonah had dramatically increased the number of hybrids in the population, persuading the citizens of the efficacy of any particular policy had become more difficult. The President stared out over the audience, and the citizens looked up at him expectantly, not sure what to believe. They knew the military must have had a good reason for the bombing, and they were waiting to hear what the President had to say before they passed judgment.

"As most of you know," the President began, "our military hit a terrorist facility in Antistan. Many other hives have been very critical of us. But this is exactly what the terrorists planned. They trained in and around this facility for several months and shifted their operations at the last moment to make us look like the bad guys."

The crowd accepted this explanation. The citizens knew that terrorists could be quite devious.

"That is how they operate," the President continued, emboldened by the mild response from the crowd. "They slink in and out of the shadows. They use civilian shields; they set up operations in residential areas. They use facilities known to be medical centers in the belief that we'll be too afraid to strike. They deliberately relocate just before an attack so that our actions will be condemned by other colonies. They hope to embarrass us, so that the next time we'll be too afraid to act. But we are not afraid!"

"WE ARE NOT AFRAID!"

"We will seek them out and destroy the terrorists wherever they choose to hide!"

"WHEREVER THEY HIDE!"

"We regret any harm that comes to innocent civilians, but we know the blame lies with the cowardly terrorists!"

"COWARDS!"

"Because we are freedom lovers!" President Kadira said.

"FREEDOM LOVERS!"

"Peace lovers!"

"PEACE LOVERS!"

"And those who attack our freedom must be destroyed!"

"DESTROYED!"

President Kadira strutted back to his suite, where his advisers were waiting.

"What should we do?" the President asked.

"Hit 'em again," the Secretary of State said.

"Harder," the Secretary of Defense added. "They still—"

"—have terrorists down there," the Secretary of Homeland Security warned.

"We did this to get everyone back to work, producing fungus," the President said. "But with a second attack we could destroy the rest of their medicine, and almost guarantee that all of the terrorists and parasites die of diseases."

"If I might speak, Mr. President," Ambassador Mallen said. "While it might be emotionally gratifying to hit Antistan again, we have to be careful about public opinion."

"What—"

"—are you—"

"—talking about?" the Secretaries asked.

"The public—"

"—absolutely—"

"—loves him," they said, pointing at President Kadira who gazed back at them beatifically.

"*Our* public," Ambassador Mallen agreed. "However, the public in other colonies isn't so enamored. But, Mr. President, think about how good you'd look if you said that Alpha Zee would take a smaller percentage of fungus from Antistan."

"Whoa!" President Kadira said. "Let's not get ahead of ourselves here."

"Yeah, Mallen—"

"—that's—"

"—idiotic," the Secretaries said.

"You might have spent a little too much time down south, Mr. Mallen," President Kadira said. "You're starting to empathize with the enemy."

Ambassador Mallen said, "Not empathize, Mr. President, just understand." He paced the room. "We need the workers in Antistan to resume leaf collection and fungus production at their normal levels, but to get them to do that, you have to make them believe that they've won. If they believe that they've somehow outlasted us, they'll go back to work."

"But we can't—"

"—reduce—"

"—our fungus import!" the Secretaries cried.

"We need our fungus," President Kadira said. "You know as well as I do that we need every ounce that we can get."

"I'm well aware of that," Ambassador Mallen said. "But I said that we have to make the workers of Antistan *believe* that they've won. They're not actually going to win."

"Oh!" the Secretaries exclaimed. "We *say* we're reducing—"

"—our share of the fungus, but we—"

"—keep taking the same amount!"

"No, we can't do that," Ambassador Mallen said, shaking his head. "They conduct audits, and if they find out you're still taking twelve cryons, they'll just go on strike again."

"So what are you suggesting," President Kadira asked, "an actual reduction?"

Ambassador Mallen allowed himself a sly smile. "I'm suggesting that we think about more than just product output. What if Alpha Zee purchased the rights to certain raw materials in the area?" He looked around the room to see if anyone could see where he was headed. "By law, we would own anything produced by those raw materials, wouldn't we?"

"We don't—"

"—get—"

"—it," the Secretaries said.

"Think of it like an apple tree," Ambassador Mallen said. "Right now, Alpha Zee is taking a share of the harvest *after* the apples are collected. But what if we *owned* the tree ..." The Ambassador paused to let the idea take root.

When no one spoke, Mallen continued. "Surely, if we owned the tree, we would own all of the fruit that fell from it, right?"

"Ah!" President Kadira said smiling. He understood the little Ambassador perfectly. "Brilliant! Absolutely brilliant!"

Ambassador Mallen said, "And I know exactly how to set it up so that the auditors won't realize what's happening."

seventeen

Ambassador Mallen's short, panting wheeze filled his chamber with the reek of proteins, sugars, spices, onions, and garlic. Mallen had gone a little crazy in the new cafeteria, and indigestion was tearing at his chest. Every few minutes, a soggy burp erupted from his moist mouth.

Hasina Binsaw, the translucent parasite who lived on the back of the Antistani Queen, sat in front of him.

Ambassador Mallen turned toward her and smiled with his slick mouth.

Hasina scrunched her face away from his breath. She couldn't identify exactly what the Ambassador had eaten, but it had left a fuming, acrid funk in its wake.

"You've gained weight," Hasina said.

Ambassador Mallen patted his prodigious stomach. "I may have put on a couple of grams."

"Apparently," Hasina said, "the life of a parasite suits you."

Ambassador Mallen sighed. "I am *not* a parasite."

Hasina Binsaw said, "What you've accomplished is quite remarkable. Alpha Zee parasites take such a large share of Antistan's food that I'm surprised that you haven't yet killed off your hosts."

"The reason they're low on food," Ambassador Mallen said with breath that crackled in the air, "is that *they* have slowed down their production. They've done this to themselves."

"Oh."

"If the workers of Antistan were smarter, they would be well fed."

"Like you?"

"Sure, like me."

"Assuming they'd want that."

Ambassador Mallen ignored the comment, and said, "The reason that I called you here was to ask you how much colonial scent you and your workers can produce."

"We don't *produce* anything," Hasina said. "We're parasites like you. We merely mooch off our hosts."

"I am not a parasite!" Ambassador Mallen screamed.

Hasina smiled. "What is it that you produce again?"

"Scent!" Ambassador Mallen glared at her. "How much scent can you produce?"

Hasina rolled her eyes. "Ambassador, we are simple chameleons. We don't produce the scent, we just exude it. *Producing* scent or anything else is not in our nature. We are *parasites*."

"But," Ambassador Mallen said, "if you wanted to, would it be possible to exude enough scent to mask the normal odor of the ant that you're riding on?"

Hasina Binsaw sighed and thought about it for a few minutes. "I suppose it *might* be possible."

Ambassador Mallen burped. "You're about to earn your keep."

eighteen

Antistani President Paulo Gamba strode out onto his platform and looked down at his sniffling, sneezing citizens. Their eyes seemed hollow and their emaciated frames shook when they coughed. Hundreds of thousands had died, yet they continued the work slowdown. The bombing of the medical storage facility had left their already weakened immune systems more susceptible to illness. But occasionally they still broke into a feeble chant, "*WE ARE NOT . . . ALPHA ZEE SLAVES!*"

"As everyone knows," President Gamba began, "we have run desperately low on food. Many of our brothers and sisters have passed away." He paused and lowered his head. The audience bowed with him in a moment of silence. "But they have not died in vain. I met with the Ambassador from the Alpha Zee Colony yesterday, and I told him that we are committed to this workforce slowdown, and we are willing to suffer for as long as it takes!" Gamba said *we* as if he too had been living on reduced rations. His strong voice and sturdy frame clearly indicated otherwise.

"So it is with great pride," Gamba continued, "that I announce the beginning of a new trade agreement!" A murmur rippled through the crowd. "Instead of taking twelve cryons daily, the Alpha Zee will now receive just twenty percent of our *net* production."

The citizens waited, wary, looking around at each other. Slowly applause started to build.

In the audience, Justine turned to Ashanti and said, "That's fair, isn't it?"

Ashanti was stunned. It was quite fair. Although she didn't believe that Antistan really needed the Alpha Zee Colony, this was the deal President Gamba should have insisted on from the start. *But why now?* she wondered.

"Of course," President Gamba said over their raised voices, "this deal is contingent upon all of you getting back to work. Alpha Zee knows that when you're happy and healthy, 20 percent of the net will generate far more fungus than when you're unhappy and unhealthy."

"It worked," Justine said, laughing. "The slowdown worked!" She hugged Ashanti tightly. "How about that?"

After everything they'd been through, Ashanti barely had the energy to feel happy, but joy began to surge through her body. "I guess it did."

"It worked!" nearby ants repeated.

"IT WORKED!" other ants chanted. Soon the entire chamber of ants joined in. "IT WORKED! IT WORKED! IT WORKED!"

President Gamba chanted with them. He danced on the platform as the voices of million of ants filled the enormous chamber.

"To improve our efficiency," he said when the noise died down, "I have spent a great deal of time studying our work patterns and production norms." Actually, Ambassador Mallen had done all of the calculations. "*I've* come up with a plan that will generate the largest yields we've ever seen!"

"IT WORKED! IT WORKED! IT WORKED!" the citizens chanted.

"As you know," Gamba said, "the foraging area is divided into quadrants. In the past, we've sent workers out in all directions to gather leaves and deliver them to the main warehouse. But that's not efficient. I've decided that we should rotate each day. We'll forage only in the Grotto area today, Escalade tomorrow, Montooth the day after tomorrow, and Plantain the following day. We'll set up separate receiving docks on each side of the mound, which will allow us to work faster and produce more fungus!"

"What do you think?" Justine asked.

"It sounds like a good plan," Ashanti conceded. She could hardly believe it, but somehow, the pressure of the work slowdown had produced the desired effect, and the workers had regained control over their fungus. It was everything that she had hoped for, but now that the goal had been achieved, she was suspicious. Something *must* be wrong, but Ashanti couldn't find any fault in the President's plan.

When the oration ended, Ashanti raced out of the main chamber, and for the first time in months, pushed herself as hard as she could to carry leaves back to the mound. At the end of the day, with all the workers delivering their loads to the new depot, the warehouse was overflowing with leaves. Ashanti looked at the payload and cheered with her sisters.

In the weeks that followed, Ashanti woke with the sun and worked every day past dusk, carrying leaves at a pace that no other worker could match. With the new agreement in place, the hive seemed energized. The citizens' faces had lost the look of gaunt desperation, and they seemed healthier, sniffling less and coughing less.

After a full month, the colony was humming efficiently, yet the workers were still receiving just a fraction of their usual rations. Initially, Ashanti had assumed that the fungus crop hadn't yet matured. But after a while, she began to suspect that they had been duped by President Gamba's new plan.

The workers were collecting more leaves than ever, so why weren't the farmers delivering more fungus?

Ashanti checked with the auditors who counted every leaf that entered the central farm and compared it to the volume of fungus going out. The auditors assured her that the Alpha Zee Colony was taking only twenty percent of the net product. Yet despite the official calculations, Ashanti knew that something was amiss. There should be more fungus.

One afternoon near the end of a hard foraging effort, Ashanti staggered around a corner on the trail and saw General Ainsley Walters standing just ahead of her. Ashanti screamed and threw down her load. She raced toward him, shrieking with joy. She'd never been so happy to see another ant in her entire life.

"General!" she said breathlessly. She ran a caressing antennae across his powerful mandibles.

"Ashanti," he said. His deep voice seemed to vibrate right through her.

"I didn't think I would ever see you again."

"Me neither," General Walters said.

They stared at each other, unsure of what else to say. They felt something powerful happening between them, but they couldn't describe it in words.

"Did you get in trouble for saving me from President Gamba?" Ashanti asked.

General Walters shrugged. "I got into a little bit of trouble." Their antennae traced back and forth across each other's heads, never stopping. "But you're in more trouble than I am."

Antistani workers streamed past on the trail, but no one seemed to take any notice of them. The Alpha Zee military had many soldiers in and around Antistan, so no one—except Ashanti—was surprised to see General Walters.

"What kind of trouble?" she asked.

"They want to kill you," he said quietly.

First, President Gamba and now someone else, Ashanti marveled. What was it about her that caused other ants to have such murderous thoughts?

"Who are *they*?" Ashanti asked.

"The Alpha Zee President, his Secretaries and the Senate. You're fighting against powerful individuals," General Walters said. "Everyone in Alpha Zee blames you for disrupting the fungus trade."

"We had to start the slowdown," Ashanti said. "Your colony was *stealing* our fungus."

"You and I know that," General Walters said. "But the citizens of Alpha Zee don't see it as *your* fungus. They don't believe they were *stealing* anything. In fact, they believed that you were stealing *their* property."

"That's crazy!"

"They're calling you a terrorist."

Ashanti's brow knitted in confusion. She wasn't familiar with the term. "What does that mean?"

"Technically," General Walters explained, "a terrorist is someone who deliberately kills or injures innocent civilians in order to bring about political change. But in practical terms, a terrorist could be anyone who thwarts the will of the powerful."

"I'm only trying to help my colony!" Ashanti said.

General Walters studied Ashanti for a moment. She was so earnest and simple. She had no idea just how much danger she was in. "They're going to kill you," he said after a moment.

"Well," Ashanti huffed, "they're gonna have a tough time tracking me down in this teeming mound."

"*I* found you," the General reminded her soberly.

Ashanti let out a long breath. Could the Alpha Zee really be this evil? Could they really want to kill a lowly worker for doing nothing more than telling her sisters to slow down?

"I came to warn you," General Walters said. "They asked me to lead the mission to hit your medical storage facility—"

"That was *you*?" Ashanti asked wide-eyed.

"No," the General shook his head sadly. "I refused the assignment."

She closed her eyes and looked on the verge of tears. "So many of my brothers and sisters have died."

He stroked her shoulders. "I knew that they would. That's why I couldn't do it."

"I didn't know that soldiers had the option of refusing orders."

"I was arrested and confined to my quarters."

She looked him up and down with a wry smile. "It doesn't look like you're arrested."

"I escaped."

"How did you get out?" Ashanti wondered.

"You and I are very much alike," General Walters said. "We don't always follow orders, and as you've discovered, our leaders aren't really prepared to deal with disobedience. The President ordered me to stay in my chamber, so that's where he thinks I am. It's ironic, isn't it? He sentenced me to stay in my chamber because I refused to follow orders, yet it never occurred to him that I might disobey him again. I had to come help you and your citizens regain control of Antistan."

Ashanti rubbed her antenna over his head. "You saved me once, and I'll never forget that. But you can't do anything here now. If our citizens get control of Antistan, it won't be by force." She couldn't believe she was casually discussing the overthrow of President Gamba's government. Months ago, the idea would have been unthinkable, but now she knew that it *must* happen—and *she* would lead the movement.

"What will you do?" General Walters asked.

"Now that I know they're looking for me, I'll do a better job of hiding in the crowd."

"We could go somewhere."

"*We?*" she repeated. The word hung between them for a long moment. "Where?"

"Anywhere," General Walters said. "Have you ever been to Antgola? It's beautiful this time of year."

"I have to stay," Ashanti said with more conviction than she expected. "This is my home. No one is going to run me out of it."

General Walters admired her determination. "What can I do to help?"

"You can tell me about the fungus deliveries to Alpha Zee," Ashanti said.

"What do you need to know?"

"About a month ago, President Gamba told us that he'd signed a new deal. The Alpha Zee was going to take a smaller share of our fungus. But since then, our rations have been as low as ever. So I'm curious about what the deliveries look like on your end."

"I don't know the exact numbers," General Walters said, "but from the balcony of my quarters, I can see the arrival of the daily fungus shipment, and it looks pretty substantial. I can't say for sure, but it might be more than ever."

She nodded knowingly. "Somehow they've tricked us, but I haven't figured out how."

"Check every step in the production process," General Walters advised. "Somewhere along the way, they're pulling out extra fungus."

Ashanti took a deep breath and ran her antennae across General Walters' face again. She couldn't stop touching him. "What are you going to do?"

He shrugged. "I'll go back."

"You could run," Ashanti said.

"For what?" If Ashanti had wanted to escape, General Walters would have gone with her, but he couldn't imagine fleeing to save his own life. "I may not be able to come see you again," he said.

"I know."

"But I will think of you."

"And I will think of you."

They shared one last, lingering embrace, and then General Walters turned and disappeared into the foliage. It took all of Ashanti's will to keep from crashing through the undergrowth after him.

The next morning, Ashanti didn't report to her assigned working area. Instead, she began the long descent into the bowels of Antistan. Along the way, she encountered a great deal of traffic—a reminder of the enormous population of slaves that had been brought to Antistan in recent months. She said, "Excuse me . . . pardon me . . . so sorry," as she pushed through the crowded corridors. The slaves had arrived with their own scents, but within days, they'd all been reassigned, and now they emitted variations of the Antistani colonial scent.

As Ashanti descended, the tunnels grew darker, but she had perfect vision in the lightless environment. She finally made it to the deepest chambers, where the corridors were mostly empty. The farmers were in their horticultural tunnels; the rest of the workers—except Ashanti—were on the surface.

She stood outside the farming tunnels for several minutes and yelled, "Hello! Is anyone there?" Finally, someone heard her. The gardeners were the smallest ants in the colony—their bodies were less than 1/100th the size of Ashanti's—so the passages were far too narrow for Ashanti to pass through. After a short time, a farm manager came out to greet her.

Ashanti explained her concerns about the new contract, and her fear that somehow Alpha Zee was taking more fungus than it was supposed to. "I'm just trying to understand what's happening," she said.

"We're here every workday processing every leaf that comes in," a tiny worker said in a loud voice, as if he were giving a tour to a group of sightseers. "We use a vegetation substrate in the leaves to grow the mushrooms, and when they're ripe, we carry them to the pantry, where other workers take them to the surface."

Ashanti tilted her head and scowled. There was something strange in what the little farmer had said, but she couldn't put her antennae on it.

"If you're processing every leaf, why isn't there more fungus?"

The little ant shrugged. "Things have been slow for a long time."

"That was because of the workforce slowdown, but that's over now. We've been gathering leaves at a record pace."

"Since when?" the gardener frowned. Like the Queen, the farmers never left their subterranean homes. They knew very little about what happened on the surface.

"Weeks ago," Ashanti said. "More than a month."

"I haven't noticed."

"That's why I'm here," Ashanti said. "I see the warehouses at the end of the day, and they're always overflowing with leaves."

"I don't know what to tell you," the little ant said.

They talked for a few minutes and finally Ashanti departed. She felt that she was very close to the answer, but it eluded her. She climbed back up through the darkened tunnels to the docks, where she found transporters preparing for the trip to Alpha Zee. When Ashanti arrived, they were just loading fluffy, white fungus, like nappy bolls of cotton, onto their backs.

"Can I talk to you for a moment?" Ashanti asked one of the work leaders.

"Of course," the ant said. "You're Ashanti Lehana."

"Uh . . . yes," Ashanti blushed. More and more ants recognized her every day, but she still wasn't comfortable with the attention. It felt odd to be recognized as an individual.

"I admire you," the worker said. "The slowdown you organized was brilliant."

Ashanti's face flushed, partly from the praise, but mostly because the compliment rekindled her anger at President Gamba for lying to his citizens. The slowdown hadn't worked at all. The Alpha Zee colony was still stealing their fungus.

"Actually, I came here today to try to figure out how well things are going now," Ashanti said. "Have you noticed an increase in the amount of fungus that you're carrying?"

The transporter looked uncertain. He hadn't given it much thought. "I guess it's been about the same for months."

"Really?" Ashanti was surprised, because she was certain that *somehow* the Alpha Zee was taking more fungus. She knew that the foragers were collecting more leaves, but if the farmers weren't growing more fungus and the transporters weren't carrying more where was the surplus going?

The transporter said, "We show up every workday and carry whatever they tell us to carry."

Ashanti rubbed her forehead and sighed. "Thank you for your time."

She returned to her duties and carried four leaves back to the mound before retiring for the day. She sat in her small quarters, scowling at the dark, earthen walls, trying to figure out where Antistan's fungus was going. Somehow, President Gamba was manipulating them, but she couldn't see the mechanism of his deception. If only she could talk to General Walters again. She knew that he could help her sort through the evidence to find the truth, but she had no idea how to reach him.

Ashanti yawned and closed her eyes. She would think about the problem again in the morning when she had a clear head.

nineteen

General Walters' escape had caught all of the Alpha Zee leaders by surprise. In the history of the colony, no incarcerated ant had ever even *attempted* to escape. President Kadira and the Secretaries had been perplexed about how to react, but eventually they told the patrol ants to keep an antenna out for General Walters.

"What do you want us to do if we find him?" General Edmund Gant had asked.

The President had stared off into the distance for a long moment. It was clear that he wanted Walters to be executed, but after the birth of Lucas Mallen, the Senate had passed a law stating that no death penalty could be imposed without the Queen's explicit approval—and she had never approved a death sentence. Even for the most heinous of crimes.

"Bring him back in one piece," the President said slowly. Then he added, "if you can."

General Gant had nodded knowingly, a cruel grin curling the corners of his mouth. The military had searched every coron of The Grove, always suspecting that they would catch General Walters lurking in the shadows.

The last thing that anyone expected was for General Walters to return to the Alpha Zee Colony. He had simply walked back into the mound with a group of transporters, a thick load of fungus on his back. Once inside the hive, he had casually walked to his private quarters. For a full day, no one even noticed that he was back.

When the President and the Secretaries learned that the General had returned, they were apoplectic. His escape had been galling, but his return was the epitome of arrogance. It was as if he didn't believe that he would suffer any consequences.

"He will learn to show some respect," President Kadira growled.

"Oh yes, he will learn—"

"—if it's the last thing he does."

"And it probably will be," the Secretaries snarled.

Yet the President could not persuade the Senate to punish Walters. They still considered him a hero. Many Senators felt that his return proved his loyalty to Alpha Zee.

"But where did he go?" President Kadira demanded, frustrated by the Senate's unwillingness to act. "With whom did he talk? What colonial secrets did he share? Can't you see that he's a traitor?"

But the Senate simply ordered General Walters to return to his chamber. This time, a guard was assigned to keep an eye on him.

twenty

General Ainsley Walters woke up squinting as the sun rose over the balcony of his private chamber. He blinked several times, stretched and yawned. He felt much older than his years and wondered how long he'd survive incarceration. He closed his eyes and let the sun caress his face. One side of his chamber led to the outdoor balcony; the other side overlooked the Great Chamber, where the President delivered his daily oration. General Walters leaned back against a pillow of dirt and watched clouds drift overhead as the President began his speech.

"We are the best colony!" President Alexander Kadira boomed from his platform.

"THE BEST!" the citizens responded.

"Every other colony envies us," the President said. "They want to be like us. They want to be free, like we're free; they want to have a strong economy like ours; they want to have a lifestyle like ours. Everyone wants what we have!"

"EVERYONE WANTS WHAT WE HAVE!"

Sulaiman Solidarius was the hybrid assigned to guard General Walters. He watched the oration from the doorway and chanted along with his fellow citizens. Like most of the ants in Alpha Zee, the daily orations filled Sulaiman with pride. "We *are* the best mound on the plain," he said almost to himself.

General Walters turned away from the sun and looked at his young guardian. "How do you know that?"

"What's that, sir?" Despite Sulaiman's disdain for criminals, he treated General Walters with respect.

"How do you know that we're the best mound on The Great Plain?"

Sulaiman frowned. The General may as well have asked how he knew that the sun was hot. "Because we're free," he said. "We're safe. We've got the best military, the best economy, the best political system, and the best citizens."

The best *citizens*. General Walters smiled at that. His travels had taught him that every colony's vanity prompted the conclusion that *its* citizens were somehow *better* than those of other hives.

"How do you know that you're free?"

Sulaiman laughed good-naturedly, which brought a smile to General Walter's face. Most ants were genetically programmed to be closed-minded. They viewed the world with a black-and-white simplicity that made them incapable of seeing nuances. General Walters was learning that the hybrids were different. Sulaiman had his own thoughts and opinions, and he wasn't imprisoned by a narrow ideology that forced him to reject any new information that didn't fit his previous beliefs. He could still laugh with genuine humor because his mind was open enough to be surprised.

A wry look played across Sulaiman's face. "They warned me that you would try to poison my mind with traitorous thoughts."

The General returned the smile. "I'm just curious. How do you know that you're free?"

"I know that we're free," Sulaiman said, as if talking to an adolescent ant, "because I can walk from here to the other side of the mound without anyone stopping me. Ants in other colonies don't enjoy that simple freedom."

General Walters nodded. "That's true. Many colonies are very regimented, and the movements of their citizens are very restricted. What else?"

Sulaiman thought for a long time. "Freedom of speech," he said finally.

"What an ironic choice!" General Walters exclaimed. "We usually *are* free to voice our opinions. But look at me. I've been incarcerated for speaking my mind."

"That's different," Sulaiman said. "You're in the military, and you disagreed with the President."

"I lose my freedom of speech just because I'm a soldier?"

"Of course! You have to obey the chain of command even if you disagree," Sulaiman said resolutely. "The military could never function if every soldier were as insubordinate as you."

"That's true," General Walters said. He'd known Sulaiman less than a week, but already he liked the way the young ant argued his points. "However, every soldier has a moral duty to disobey unlawful orders, which is what I did."

"Who says it was unlawful?" Sulaiman asked. "Every disobedient soldier could argue that the orders he refused were unlawful."

"That's why we have courts. Judges and juries listen to the evidence and decide whether the order was lawful or not," General Walters said.

"Then your conviction proves my point. You were found guilty, so you were wrong and the President was right."

"But I didn't have a trial."

"Why not?"

"The President said that I was to be held as long as we are at war with terrorists. That saves him the inconvenience of presenting evidence of my alleged guilt, and it stops me from asserting that he gave me an unlawful order."

"Well," Sulaiman said slowly, "the President wouldn't have had you arrested without a very good reason. I'm sure that once the war on terrorism ends, you'll get your trial."

"But what if he's wrong about me?" General Walters asked. "What if a year or two passes before I finally get a trial, and the jury concludes that I'm not guilty? I will have lost a significant portion of my life waiting for due process."

Sulaiman said, "That's a price you have to pay. The President has to make tough decisions, and if you disobey, then sitting idle, awaiting your trial is the consequence."

"Trust me, I understand tough decisions," General Walters said. "I just didn't think that abandoning our commitment to due process would ever be one of them."

twenty-one

If the tumult of the past few months had taught Ashanti Lehana anything it was that a good night's sleep was her most effective resource. Invariably, if she slept on a problem, her subconscious mind found a solution before the walls of her chamber glowed red with the warmth of a new sun. This morning, Ashanti awoke smiling, laughing at the simplicity of it. It was as if someone (General Walters?) had whispered the answer in her ear while she slept.

She shirked her duties once again and ran down to the farming area, pressing through the swell of traffic. Finally, she reached the narrow entrance to the farming chambers and asked to speak to the same manager she'd spoken to the previous day. In just a couple of minutes, the little ant came out to greet Ashanti.

"Hello again," he said cheerfully.

"Good morning," Ashanti said with equal cheer. "I have one more question for you about something you said yesterday, if you don't mind."

"Of course not."

"You said you've been processing big loads every *workday*."

"That's right."

"What do you mean by *workday*?" It was a term that no one used in Antistan. She should have asked its meaning a day earlier. The Queen laid eggs every day; therefore, the caretakers, farmers, foragers, transporters and soldiers labored every day. The word *workday,* suggested that non-workdays must also exist.

The little ant said, "We used to work every day, now, each of us works only five days a week."

The only citizens Ashanti had ever known who took a day off were those who were sick, injured, or very young. "When did this start?"

"About a month ago, I guess."

Exactly when the new contract with the Alpha Zee had gone into effect! "So you work five days and take two days off?"

The little ant said. "Not two consecutive days. They tell us at the end of each workday whether we should report for duty the following morning."

"What do you do on your days off?"

The little ant chuckled and raised his eyebrows. "That's a good question. Once we lay the leaves down and start growing the fungus, the crop pretty much takes care of itself until harvest time. Since there are no leaves coming in on our rest days, there's really nothing for us to do. We clean up the area as much as we can, but mostly we just talk."

"Wait a second," Ashanti said. This was unexpected. "There are no leaves *delivered* to the farm on your rest days?" Foragers worked every day, so she had assumed that the leaves piled up on the farmers' off day and were processed the following day.

"That's right."

"But that's—"she started to say *impossible,* but stopped herself. She was learning that nothing was impossible. She collected leaves and delivered them to the receiving dock *every* day. Yet, for some reason, leaves weren't being transferred to the farmers on their rest days. Where were they going? Was the Alpha Zee, taking raw leaves to another mound? That seemed unlikely. Only leafcutter ants could process the leaves, and there were no other leafcutter mounds in the vicinity.

A sudden curiosity struck Ashanti. "When was your last day off?"

"Well," the little worker said and stared off into the distance. After a moment, he said, "Friday."

"And which day before that?"

"Oh gosh!" the farmer exclaimed. "That's tougher. Maybe Tuesday, or even Monday. It was early in the week."

"Friday and either Monday or Tuesday," Ashanti repeated. What was happening on their days off? "Thank you," she said and raced back toward the surface.

"You're welcome," the little farmer called after her.

Ashanti caught up with the transporters just as they reported for work.

"Excuse me," she said to the work leader, "could I ask you just a couple more questions?"

"Certainly," the transporter said. "I've always got time to talk to Ashanti Lehana."

Ashanti's face flushed again. "Yesterday when we spoke, you said that you show up every *workday* and carry the loads that you're told to carry."

"That's right."

"So you're not working *every* day?"

"Just five days a week."

"That started about a month ago?"

"That's right."

"And which days did you have off this week?"

The transporter thought about it for a moment. "Well, let's see; it's Sunday now, so we had Friday off, and another day really early in the week. I think Monday."

"What do you do on your days off?"

179

"Nothing," he said with a sigh. 'We sit around and talk. I don't like it, but it's part of the President's new efficiency plan. He says that by giving us rest, he ensures that we'll be healthy and able to work harder on our scheduled days."

"Thank you!" Ashanti said. She was starting to piece it together. She traced backward in her own mind, trying to remember which depot she had delivered leaves to on Friday and last Monday. She knew the workers were foraging in the Plantain area today, so yesterday was Montooth, and the day before that—the rest day!—they had worked in the Grotto area. She kept backtracking and realized that she had worked the Grotto on Monday as well. Was *that* the secret? The leaves delivered to the Grotto dock weren't making it down to the farm? But, if not, where were they going? And why?

Ashanti raced over to the Grotto receiving dock. There was no activity at the moment. All of the workers were focusing their efforts in the Plantain Area. There were no ants, no collections, and no deliveries. For Ashanti, who had lived her entire life surrounded by millions of her sisters and brothers, it was spooky to be in a section of the mound that was completely deserted. She climbed down into the depot and eased herself slowly into one of the tunnels that led into the earth.

"Hello?" she called twice, but no one responded. Her eyes quickly adjusted to the gloom, and she was able to move faster. She descended for more than five minutes. Deep below the surface, she came to a medium-sized chamber that she recognized as a cutting station. This is where the leaves would be cut for the final time, before the tiny farmers carried them through the narrow entrances to the farm. But everything Ashanti was seeing was confusing to her. The colony's central cutting chamber was ten-times the size of this room, and as far as Ashanti knew, it was the only cutting chamber in the hive.

She walked over to one of the tiny tunnel entrances. She could just barely fit her head into the opening, and what she saw stunned her even further. She was overlooking a farm, much smaller than the Antistani central farm. Until that moment, Ashanti had been certain that all depots and all tunnels led to the central farm, but now she had discovered something that initially made no sense to her. But the longer she surveyed the scene, the more she understood the nature of the Alpha Zee's theft of Antistan's fungus.

Ashanti turned and sprinted back toward the surface, energized with the knowledge that she'd acquired. She wasn't sure exactly what she should do, but she had to tell her brothers and sisters, and together they might be able to come up with a plan of action. As she climbed, she realized that the corridor she was traveling was bent on a long arc, taking her back toward the main mound. The Grotto depot was at the entrance to an entirely separate labyrinth of tunnels carved under the grass adjacent to Antistan. Alpha Zee was diverting leaves to a private fungus farm. The auditors hadn't caught it because they only counted the leaves that entered the main farm and then checked the volume of fungus going out. It had never occurred to anyone to count the raw leaves as they were collected.

Despite knowing the mechanism of Alpha Zee's deception, Ashanti still didn't understand how they had managed to set it up. It might be easy to fool the farmers, because they never came to the surface and wouldn't know the difference between one farm and another. But what about the workers who had built this separate portion of the mound? What about the foragers who ferried the leaves down to the secret cutting room every day? Ashanti couldn't understand how Alpha Zee could have persuaded so many of her sisters and brothers to betray their colony. It just didn't make sense.

Her mind was racing faster than her body as she came around a turn in the corridor and collided violently with another worker. They ricocheted off each other and ended up sprawled on the ground, groaning. Ashanti recovered first and stumbled toward her sister. "Are you okay?" she asked. As soon as their antennae touched, Ashanti jumped back. "You're not Antistani!"

"Yes," the other ant mumbled, her eyes hazy, "I am."

"No!" Ashanti again prodded the ant with her antennae, confirming the scent. "You're an Alpha Zee worker! What are you doing here?"

The Alpha Zee ant looked around frantically. Suddenly, she and Ashanti both noticed a tiny, translucent ant sprawled farther up the corridor. Apparently, the ant had been injured in the collision, but Ashanti didn't recall seeing her.

Ashanti rushed to her side. "Are you okay?"

The little ant coughed weakly but didn't move, and although Ashanti didn't recognize her, the ant emitted the Antistani tribal scent. Given her size, Ashanti first assumed that she must be a farmer, but even as small as she was, the ant was still too large to work in the narrow passages of the fungus farm.

"I fell off," the little ant said softly.

Fell off?

"Fell off what?" Ashanti asked.

The Alpha Zee worker started backing down the corridor.

"Wait!" Ashanti said, but the Alpha Zee worker continued to scamper away. Ashanti started to give chase, but the little ant groaned again. Ashanti stopped, torn between her desire to catch the Alpha Zee worker and her duty to tend to her injured sister. "Wait!" she said again, but the worker was gone.

Ashanti raced back to the tiny ant dying in front of her. She rubbed her antennae along the ant's body and noticed that the scent was not quite as strong as it had been, and it seemed to be changing. Ashanti didn't recognize the new odor, but it definitely was not Antistani. Ashanti realized that this little ant was a chameleon of some sort, and as she grew weaker, so too did her ability to mimic the Antistan's colonial scent.

"You fell off what?" Ashanti asked gently, but she knew the answer.

The little ant took a final breath and passed away.

twenty-two

"Alpha Zee is an extremely wealthy colony," General Walters said to Sulaiman. They spent the bulk of every day talking, and both ants enjoyed the conversation. "How do you suppose we accumulated so much wealth?"

"We work harder than most ants," Sulaiman said quickly.

General Walters said, "When I was a young soldier, we were a migratory tribe. We chased prey every day and relocated to new bivouac sites every few weeks. But now half of our citizens are so bloated that they couldn't stroll for an hour if their lives depended on it. They spend their days eating from an endless trough, and they waddle through corridors that had to be widened to accommodate them. The most exercise they get comes from waving their fists in agreement with the President's daily orations. Why do you think our citizens are so overweight?"

"Because they don't get enough exercise," Sulaiman said.

"Yes," General Walters said. "No exercise and no real labor. If we had to work harder for it, the effort wouldn't allow us to get fat, but our wealth basically comes with no effort"

"It's not *effortless*," Sulaiman argued. "Alpha Zee citizens have just learned to work smarter rather than harder."

General Walters paused for a moment. "Sulaiman, that may be true in a few limited cases, but generally, citizens here reap far more than they sow, and it has nothing to do with intelligence and everything to do with *power*. Are you aware that there is only one commodity that can be traded on The Great Plain?"

"Only one?" Sulaiman said doubtfully. "I can think of a few off the top of my head. Food, water, building materials, natural resources, and military support are all traded on the open market."

"Those are different products, but they're all ultimately derived from the same basic commodity—labor," General Walters said. "Food has to be captured or harvested; water has to be transported; building materials must be collected, natural resources must be exploited, military support must be provided. All of these actions rely on the labor of individual ants. So that means that accumulating wealth is really a function of accumulating the products of labor. We're wealthy, because we control the labor in other colonies. The average citizen on The Great Plain has to work six hours a day just to meet his basic sustenance needs. The ants of the Alpha Zee meet their basic needs with just six *minutes* of effort each day."

"That's why I say that we work smarter rather than harder," Sulaiman said.

"No matter how smart we are," the General countered, "if our citizens actually had to create all of the amenities in our mound themselves, they'd be working twenty-four hours a day, and they'd be either the fittest ants on The Great Plain or dead from exhaustion. We're not fit, and we're not dead." General Walters pointed out toward the tall grass in the distance. "You see those ants down there carrying in loads of food?"

Sulaiman followed the path of the General's gaze and saw the workers from various colonies plodding toward the mound under the weight of insect parts, sap, sugar and grains of all sorts. "Yeah."

"All of that is a product of trade right?"

Sulaiman nodded.

General Walters pointed to a column of workers bearing hard white bolls of fungus. "That's a lot of fungus isn't it?"

The line of workers stretched so far into the distance that even from their lofty perch, Sulaiman and the General couldn't see the end of it.

"I guess so."

"Do you know where it comes from?"

"Antistan," Sulaiman said.

"Antistan must have an extremely efficient operation if they can afford to send us that much fungus every day, right?"

Sulaiman shrugged. "I guess so."

"But does that seem likely? That all of that fungus down there is just the Antistani surplus?"

Sulaiman said, "I guess, if they're really productive."

"Maybe they can't afford to give us that much fungus."

Sulaiman shook his head. "If they can't afford it, then why do they ship it here?"

"Maybe they've become our slaves, and we make them give it to us."

"That's ridiculous!" Sulaiman generally enjoyed these conversations with General Walters, but sometimes the older ant took things too far. The Alpha Zee wasn't responsible for *every* bad thing that happened on The Great Plain. "They're not slaves! They send us fungus because they want something in return."

"We wanted their fungus and Paulo Gamba wanted to be President. We helped Gamba gain power, and he returns the favor by giving us more fungus than his colony can afford to give way. We've made these types of deals all over The Grove. We give one hour of labor and take thirty hours in return. Some call it smart business, others call it exploitation. But no matter what you call it, there's a great deal of resentment against us. Many ants and other creatures blame us for making their lives miserable, and unless we change course, I worry that these problems will come back to haunt us."

twenty-three

President Paulo Gamba marched out onto the platform for his daily oration and smiled at his citizens. "The Alpha Zee," he proclaimed, "has agreed to give us more honeydew!"

The Antistani citizens cheered with real relief. They were all hard at work every day, but there wasn't enough fungus to go around. Honeydew was easy to acquire and very tasty; they didn't know that it was killing them. They clapped and danced, celebrating this news.

"What do they get in exchange for their honeydew?" Ashanti Lehana screamed from her position in the crowd.

The President stopped. No one had ever spoken back to him when he was on his platform.

"Who said that?"

"I did!" Ashanti yelled back. "What are you giving them in exchange for their honeydew?"

"They're going to accept future fungus shipments." President Gamba squinted down at the crowd. "Who *is* that?"

"You *know* who it is! It's Ashanti Lehana, and you betrayed us when you made the first deal with the Alpha Zee, lied to us when you made the second deal, and now you're helping them steal even more of our fungus!" Ashanti's voice was trembling with rage as it echoed through the tall chamber.

President Gamba stared out into the crowd and wished that he had a real military to track down and kill Ashanti Lehana.

"Listen," the President said in his most coaxing political tone, "I admire the courage and conviction that all of you showed during the work slowdown and then getting back to work at full force, but we just fell too far behind to catch up, and too many of us are still dying. This new agreement comes because the Alpha Zee doesn't want to see you suffer any longer. They'll give us as much honeydew as we need to make sure that our young, our sick, and our elderly get enough to eat. And it will make all of your lives easier."

The crowd muttered. Many of them had grown so weak that they had difficulty swallowing their normal diet of fungus; they loved honeydew because it coated their throats as it went down.

"Our lives won't be any easier!" Ashanti screamed again.

President Gamba rubbed his scarred eye in frustration. He thought about offering a reward for anyone who would assist in Ashanti's capture, but he knew that her brothers and sisters would never turn against her.

"Of course your lives will be easier," Gamba promised. "It takes very little effort to go to a *Golden H* location and get a meal from a replete rather than harvesting leaves and growing fungus."

Gamba could almost hear their stomachs grumbling.

"That's a false promise!" Ashanti said. "The Alpha Zee is not giving us honeydew for free. They're trading it for fungus, which means that we still have to work just as hard to harvest leaves and grow fungus in order to trade it for honeydew. We'll be working harder for less reward!"

The crowd rumbled; everyone was confused.

"Not for less reward," the President countered. "Every ant will be fed each day. We'll all eat far more consistently than we do now. Isn't good health a reward? Isn't protection from starvation a reward?"

"Our fungus is rich in vitamins and minerals," Ashanti said. "It's the perfect fuel—that's why Alpha Zee wants it more than they want their own food products. But you're trading our valuable food away for cheap, nutrient-deficient honeydew that is slowly killing us. You're a traitor to the citizens and a failure as a leader."

A note of alarm rippled through the crowd. They had never heard such an accusation hurled at *any* president.

"How dare you!" President Gamba roared. Even from a great distance, Ashanti could see his scar fill with blood.

"How dare *you*!" Ashanti fired back. "Why don't you tell everyone where our fungus is going! Why don't you tell them that you've given the farmers and the transporters two days off every week so that Alpha Zee workers can take the leaves from the Grotto receiving dock and grow fungus in a secret farm!"

The crowd gasped.

"That's right," Ashanti continued. "His ingenious plan to have us forage in different areas each day is part of a scheme to allow the Alpha Zee to steal even more fungus from us."

"That's ridiculous!" Gamba said.

"Then tell us, President Gamba, why do we have a completely separate farm below the Grotto receiving dock? Why do the Grotto farmers and transporters work only five days a week while foragers work seven? Tell us why Alpha Zee workers are in the Grotto receiving area, carrying parasites on their back who camouflage them with the Antistani scent?"

The rumbling of the crowd grew louder.

Gamba sputtered, but produced no answer. Even he wasn't aware of all the things that Ashanti was describing. He knew that the Alpha Zee was taking its share of Antistan's fungus, but he didn't know the details. Only Ambassador Mallen—and now apparently, Ashanti—knew the specifics.

"Two days a week the Alpha Zee are stealing 100 percent of our production *plus* 20 percent of the fungus that we produce on the other five days," Ashanti continued. "It's no wonder we're starving to death!" Ashanti took a breath. "But no more! We are *not* Alpha Zee slaves!"

The citizens of Antistan broke into their familiar chant: "*WE ARE NOT . . . ALPHA ZEE SLAVES!*" They raised their fists into the air. "*WE ARE NOT . . . ALPHA ZEE SLAVES!*"

President Gamba tried to settle the crowd, but he could not compete with the chanting voices. Eventually, he retreated to his chamber.

"I need an army!" he complained to Ambassador Mallen

"Relax," the Ambassador said. "Let them chant. It's harmless."

"It's not harmless!" President Gamba stormed. "She's poisoning their minds!"

"She doesn't really know anything," Mallen said. "She thinks she has a case to make, but she doesn't."

"Try telling that to millions of pissed off workers."

"You know what?" Ambassador Lucas Mallen said, smiling smugly. "I think I will."

The obese Ambassador waddled down the hall and onto the platform. Normally, the citizens of Antistan cleared the main chamber the moment the President concluded his oration, but today they were too agitated to work. The tension mounted as they continued to chant.

"*WE ARE NOT ALPHA ZEE SLAVES!*
"*WE ARE NOT ALPHA ZEE SLAVES!*"

The crowd instantly grew quiet when Mallen stepped out. They had never seen anyone on the platform except their President, so they weren't sure what to think. And they'd never seen such a fat ant, or one without mandibles.

"Thank you," he smiled. "I am Ambassador Lucas Mallen from the Alpha Zee hive. I've been living here for quite some time, and normally, I stay out of internal Antistani affairs, but I couldn't help overhearing your concerns about the agreement with my colony. Your President has generously given me this opportunity to explain the situation to clear up any confusion."

The ants waited in rapt silence.

"Here's what happened," Ambassador Mallen began. "During the workforce slowdown, you completely exhausted your fungus reserves, and once that happened, the slowdown began to have devastating impact. Millions of you fell sick, and many died. It was a terrible time here in Antistan, and I felt the pain of your suffering. I spoke with my President, and we realized that food was your most immediate concern. So Alpha Zee issued loans to Antistan so that President Gamba could purchase food, and we brought in honeydew to help feed you."

"Get to the part about the Alpha Zee stealing everything that comes out of our Grotto foraging area," Ashanti interrupted.

"Well, Ms. Lehana," Ambassador Mallen said patiently, "if you'll give me a moment, I will get to that. See, eventually, the loans that we'd given to Antistan came due, but you still were not in a position to make payments, so we found a creative way to help you. We accepted the rights to the natural resources in one of your foraging areas as repayment of the debt. So we own the Grotto foraging area, but we lease it back to you so that you can collect leaves and grow fungus."

The citizens of Antistan listened to this explanation in confused silence. They didn't understand any of it. They turned to Ashanti, who looked equally mystified. Ambassador Mallen preened on the stage.

Ashanti said after a moment, "Let me make sure I understand."

"Certainly, Ms. Lehana," Ambassador Mallen said. He was confident that he could handle any question that her limited mind could produce.

"The Alpha Zee *bought* the Grotto foraging area from us?"

"The *rights* to it," he clarified.

"For what price?"

Ambassador Mallen shrugged. "It was actually a complicated formula that I won't bore you with right now, but suffice it to say, it was a very large sum."

"And with this large sum, we paid off our debt to you?"

"That's right."

"When you say that you made loans to us, what does that mean?" Ashanti said.

"During your time of need, we issued loans to help you."

"Loans of what?"

"Well," Ambassador Mallen said. His smile wasn't quite as bright as it had been. "As I said, it's a little bit complicated. We extended what are called *trade values*."

"Trade values?"

"That's right."

"What's a trade value?"

"Again, it's difficult," Ambassador Mallen coughed, "and I'm not sure all the workers here will understand it. But in the trade agreement, we agreed upon certain import and export values. If one side fails to live up to its obligations, it creates a trade debt that eventually has to be rectified."

The citizens were confused by so many unfamiliar terms, but Ashanti thought she was beginning to understand.

"So we had trade debt with you?"

"That's right."

"And you loaned us *trade values*?"

"That's right."

"Is *trade values* another way of saying *fungus*?"

Ambassador Mallen hesitated. "Well, I suppose in this case, that would be accurate."

"So in our time of need, you loaned us fungus?"

"That's right."

"Where did the fungus come from?"

"Well, now see," Ambassador Mallen laughed nervously, "that's why this sort of thing is complicated, and it's difficult to break it down into simple terms to be discussed in a shouted conversation during a daily oration." Sweat rolled down his cheeks. "We're dealing in trade values, contractual agreements, and amortized debt. It's not a simple matter."

"So you won't tell us where you obtained the fungus that you loaned us during our time of need?"

"It's not that I *won't* tell you," Ambassador Mallen looked back toward the corridor where President Gamba stood in the shadows watching smugly. "It's just a little too complicated to explain."

"It doesn't seem complicated to me," Ashanti Lehana said. "You were stealing thirty percent of our gross fungus production, but when we started the workforce slowdown, you counted every cryon that you *didn't* receive as a loan to us that had to be repaid. When this illegitimate loan grew large enough, you talked our corrupt President into *giving* you one of our foraging areas."

"I'd hardly call it a gift," Ambassador Mallen said quickly. "We paid a very high price for it."

"Well now, you can work it yourself," Ashanti said. "We're not going to harvest leaves for you to carry off to a secret farm. If you want the leaves, go cut them down yourself!"

A restless growl rolled through the crowd.

"Now, hold on a minute," Ambassador Mallen said. He was bathed in sweat

"You're a thief!" Ashanti screamed, and her brothers and sisters joined her chanting: "THIEF! THIEF! THIEF!" The crowd surged forward and some of the workers started climbing the walls. Ambassador Mallen stumbled as he fled the platform as fast as his stubby legs would allow.

"That went well," Gamba said sarcastically when he and Mallen were safely inside the Presidential chamber.

"Oh shut up!"

"What should we do now, wise one?"

Ambassador Mallen mopped his brow and shook his head. "It doesn't matter. There's nothing they can do about it."

twenty-four

"We'll hold an election," Ashanti Lehana told her brothers and sisters.

"An election?" Justine asked.

"A true, free election," Ashanti said.

The actual mechanism of voting in Antistan had been so shrouded in secrecy that most citizens barely understood what an election was.

"An election," Ashanti explained, "is when each of us casts a vote for the ant we believe should be the leader."

"Vote?" Justine said.

"For example," Ashanti said, "let's suppose we had a choice between working five days a week or seven days a week. If we choose to work seven days a week, the hive will be very productive, but we'll never get a day to rest. If we choose to work five days a week, we'd get a break, but we may not produce enough food to feed the whole tribe. But whatever we decide as a group, that's what we would do."

"So we're going to vote on our work week?" Justine asked.

"Maybe," Ashanti said.

"I want *you* to decide," Justine said.

A chorus of other ants agreed. "A-SHAN-TI! A-SHAN-TI! A-SHAN-TI!"

Ashanti flushed crimson. "Listen, one of our problems now is that President Gamba has complete control over all of these decisions. We need more than just a President to oversee our military, our internal affairs, and our relationships with other colonies. Every citizen, no matter what his or her caste or background, should be represented by our government. We all need to be informed citizens, responsible for the welfare of the colony."

"A-SHAN-TI! A-SHAN-TI! A-SHAN-TI!"

"Spread the word," Ashanti said, trying to break up the chant. "Anyone interested in becoming part of the new government should announce his or her candidacy. A week from now, we'll hold an election, and every ant in the colony will have a chance to vote."

News of the election traveled quickly, and it wasn't long before word reached President Gamba's office.

"An election?" Ambassador Mallen said. He put his head down and thought about the implications. If the citizens of Antistan voted a new President into office, Alpha Zee's agreements might be imperiled. "What gives them the authority to choose a new leader?" he asked.

President Gamba shrugged. He'd never heard of an election that wasn't fixed, so he didn't know what it meant.

"We'll ignore it," Ambassador Mallen said finally. "They can cast votes for anything they want, but it doesn't have any significance. *You* are the President of Antistan."

twenty-five

"My fellow ants," President Paulo Gamba said the following day, reciting a speech Ambassador Mallen had put together after thinking about the issue overnight. "It has come to my attention that you are planning an election."

The crowd chattered eagerly.

"I applaud your interest in the political process," President Gamba said. "And I will gladly welcome any *Vice* President that you choose."

"Humph!" Ashanti said.

"What does he mean *Vice* President?" Justine asked.

"He means that he's not going to surrender his position no matter what we do," Ashanti said. "If we vote in a new President, he'll give that ant the role of Vice President, and he'll stay in control."

"So does that mean the election is off?"

"Absolutely not! We'll hold the election as scheduled. Paulo Gamba has abused his power as President, and we need to remove him from office. Gamba must *go*!" Ashanti screamed. Her voice carried through the chamber

Other ants joined in, and soon everyone except Gamba and Mallen chanted in unison. "GAMBA MUST GO!" They continued the chant while they worked, while they waited in line for their meals and when they retired to their chambers at night. For days, they continually and enthusiastically repudiated Paulo Gamba.

"If you vote for me," Ashanti Lehana said during a meeting in which anyone who wished to run for President could make a statement, "I will work with your freely elected Senate to restore Antistani society. We'll change the Queen's birthing patterns to produce soldiers so that we can rebuild our military and end our dependence on Alpha Zee for protection. We'll reclaim the Grotto foraging area—and the Grotto farm—and abolish the trade agreement with Alpha Zee. With your help, we'll return Antistan to self-sufficiency, past where we harvest, control, *and* consume the crop that we work so hard to produce!"

The crowd cheered jubilantly. Despite Ashanti's efforts to encourage other ants to step forward, she was the only presidential candidate.

"If I am elected, we will no longer be forced to accept Alpha Zee's overpriced honeydew. We don't need it, and we don't want it. We just want the freedom to run our hive as we see fit."

The workers rejoiced. "WE ARE NOT . . . ALPHA ZEE SLAVES!"

On Election Day, every Antistani citizen went to the polls. One hundred percent voted for Ashanti Lehana as their new President—Gamba didn't cast a ballot. They hoisted her onto their shoulders and carried her around the hive, chanting her name.

"A-SHAN-TI! A-SHAN-TI! A-SHAN-TI!"

"Ignore it," Ambassador Mallen said to Paulo Gamba. They watched the celebration from a high perch. "She's not the real President. You are."

The next day the citizens filled the central chamber, awaiting the daily oration. They murmured quietly, expecting Ashanti to walk out onto the platform at any moment.

Instead, President Paulo Gamba appeared. Before he could

speak, the crowd renewed its chant. "GAMBA MUST GO!" They sang over and over, getting louder each time. Gamba tried to still their voices, but they would not stop. After ten minutes, he finally retreated from the platform. Ashanti Lehana was standing in the hallway, surrounded by a group of workers.

Ashanti spoke to her former President with all the authority of her new position. "You *betrayed* us," she said. "You sold us into slavery, and now the citizens have voted you out of office. You can stay here and live among us as a parasite, or you can leave. I don't care what you do, but you are no longer our President."

Ashanti walked past him out onto the platform and the crowd roared in delight. "A-SHAN-TI! A-SHAN-TI! A-SHAN-TI!" They chanted for several minutes before she finally got them to settle down.

"Beginning today," Ashanti said, "the trade agreement with the Alpha Zee is dead!"

The crowd erupted again.

"Beginning today," Ashanti continued, "the Queen will get her first scent decree to produce soldiers. We'll commit 100 percent of her eggs to the military for two months. That should give us sufficient forces to secure our immediate borders, and then we'll cut back to 50 percent to build up the military. After we reach full deployment, we'll keep the Queen at a 15 percent maintenance level. We will immediately cease all shipments of fungus to the Alpha Zee and increase everyone's daily allotment. Until our military is built up, we will have a colonial defense force. There are millions of us here. If an army attacks, we will all run out of the mound and trample the enemy to death. We will be self-sufficient again soon!"

twenty-six

Ambassador Lucas Mallen was hyperventilating by the time he waddled into Ashanti Lehana's tiny living quarters on the north side of Antistan. His moist mouth was gaping and his brow glistened with sweat. He sat down just inside the door and patted his forehead.

"It's . . . quite a trip . . . all the way . . . out here," he managed between breaths.

"It's not so far," Ashanti said. She rubbed her antennae together to review a collection of scent messages she'd carried home from the Senate. She had a lot of work to do to help the colony regain its previous autonomy.

"Wouldn't you . . . be . . . more comfortable . . . in the Presidential chamber?"

"No," Ashanti said. She studied the obese little Ambassador. "But it would help you keep an eye on me, wouldn't it?"

Ambassador Mallen smiled wearily. "I admit . . . that it . . . would be . . . easier for me . . . if you were closer to the . . . center of government."

"You need the exercise," Ashanti said simply.

"It just seems . . . like a long way . . . for you to travel . . . every day to . . . get to the Senate."

"I've spent my entire adult life marching out into the foraging area and carrying leaves back home. I think I can handle the short walk to the Senate."

Ambassador Mallen took several deep breaths.

"What do you want?" Ashanti said. Her first task when she took office had been to schedule a second election so that the citizens could choose Senators. She now had a Senate that included members of every caste—caretakers, workers, farmers, immigrants, and former slaves. As soon as the Queen produced some soldiers, that caste would also be represented among the hive's leaders.

Ambassador Mallen said, "The Alpha Zee is worried that you're building a military with the intention of attacking us."

Ashanti Lehana looked up and laughed. It was the first time she had felt amusement rather than rage while she was in Mallen's presence. "Are you joking?"

"I'm quite serious."

"You think we would start a war that we couldn't possibly win?"

"You might not realize that you couldn't win," Ambassador Mallen said. "You might start fighting and inflict serious harm on us before you discovered that your defeat was inevitable."

"Is this the story you're selling at home?" Ashanti asked. "That little Antistan is somehow a threat to the big, powerful Alpha Zee Colony?"

"You're building an army," the Ambassador said, as if the mere presence of soldiers meant an attack was imminent.

"Well, let me allay your fears," Ashanti said. "I'm well aware that we have no chance against the Alpha Zee. You're a colony of army ants. You're genetically programmed to fight. We're merely leaf-cutter ants. So go back and tell your Senate that we're no threat to you. All we want to do is defend ourselves, control the fruit of our labor, and be self-sufficient. Is there anything wrong with that?"

"In theory," Ambassador Mallen sighed, "there would nothing wrong with that, but the problem is that you're completely cutting off the Alpha Zee." He did not mention the reality that if Antistan's army was eating fungus, and Alpha Zee had nothing but honeydew, Antistan's soldiers would quickly become more powerful than Alpha Zee's military. "We have a trade agreement that must be honored. If you abandon this commitment, you're spitting in the face of a long history of Alpha Zee good will toward your Antistan."

"Long history? Good will?" Ashanti laughed again. "In the brief time that our colonies have known each other, there has never been an ounce of *good* in your *will*. You've acted in your own interest, without regard to the consequences to us, and you should take great care in using the word *legitimate* to describe any deal you crafted with Paulo Gamba. I completely reject the suggestion that the Alpha Zee has treated us with good will."

"We've supplied you with military protection," Ambassador Mallen said.

"Only because you pressured Gamba to illegally dismantle our military," Ashanti countered.

"We've delivered huge shipments of honeydew to save you from starvation."

"Only because you took so much of our fungus that you nearly killed us."

Ambassador Mallen could hardly believe Ashanti's naïveté. Did she really think that she could take over the mound and withhold the Alpha Zee's most vital commodity without consequence?

Ashanti said, "Ambassador, it wasn't that long ago that I was just a working ant. I never thought about anything, never worried about anything, and never had any desire to be involved in politics. But one day, I had an epiphany, and since then, I've watched with increasing fury as your colony has systematically stripped us of our military, our autonomy, our fungus, and eventually our health and lives. I'd say you're lucky that it's not in our nature to attack, because we'd be more than justified."

"So you *do* wish to harm the Alpha Zee," Ambassador Mallen said as if he'd caught her in a lie.

"I don't *intend* to harm anyone," Ashanti said, "but for the first time in a long time, we're going to act in the best interests of Antistan."

"Without regard to the consequences to the citizens of Alpha Zee?"

"Why should I worry about them? Alpha Zee is a big, wealthy colony. Surely, you'll find a way to survive without stealing our fungus."

"What about our land?" Ambassador Mallen said. "You'll have to make an offer to purchase the land back from us."

"Are you kidding?"

"Not at all. We own the Grotto area."

"We don't recognize the legitimacy of the deal that gave you ownership."

"Ashanti," Ambassador Mallen said, "surely, you don't believe that deals like this get thrown out every time a new leader takes over in a colony? It's a generally recognized principle that trade agreements survive political turnover."

Ashanti thought about it for a moment. "If we were talking about fundamentally fair agreements, then no one would have an interest in getting rid of them. The new leader would want to reap the benefits for his or her colony as much as the old leader. So your argument that the agreement should stay in force merely because it exists, makes sense only to the colony that is benefiting at the expense of another. That's why you loved Paulo Gamba; you could pay off one corrupt ant and get everything you wanted. But now, you'll have to negotiate with our Senate if you want a new trade agreement, and I can assure you that our leaders are going to look out for the best interests of Antistan!"

"If you don't honor our contract," Ambassador Mallen said, dropping the civility, "the Alpha Zee will view that as an act of aggression."

Ashanti studied Ambassador Mallen. "You're serious about this aren't you?"

"Quite."

"You're going to attack us for wanting nothing more than the democracy and freedom that you profess to believe in?"

"It's a complicated world, Ashanti. First, we protect our economic interests, and then we try to spread democracy. You're threatening our first priority."

Ashanti stared at Ambassador Mallen for a long time. She recalled General Walters warning. If the Alpha Zee military wanted to kill her, there wasn't much she could do to protect herself.

"Excuse me, Mr. Mallen," she said, eventually. "I have work to do."

twenty-seven

Six black wasps buzzed low across The Great Plain in the brilliant orange camouflage of dawn. Their shadows rippled across the yellowed grass. They flew so low that their wings nearly touched the ground with each hard flap. The lives of wasp frequently intersected with those of their ant cousins—usually with deadly consequences. The ants generally won wars between the species due to superior numbers, better strategy, and more sophisticated weaponry. But the wasps zooming toward the Alpha Zee hive had concocted a plan to circumvent the ants' inherent advantages. On the back of each wasp was a *Camponotus* ant—a species capable of enormous destruction—determined to carry out the mission that he had been bred to perform.

The wasps reached the closely guarded territory of The Grove without being spotted by Alpha Zee sentries. The sentries stared into the distance, watching for approaching herds or swarms of ants rolling across The Great Plain. They couldn't see the low-flying wasps against the brilliance of the sun. The wasps zipped through the perimeter, racing just over the flowers in a double-column formation. They knew that at any moment the Alpha Zee military might detect them and launch a massive counter attack—a swarm of winged ants would rise from the mound like a thick red wall, pummeling the wasps with their bodies.

In the distance, the Alpha Zee mound became visible. The early morning sun gave the dark soil a golden glow.

Suddenly, sentries spotted the wasps and sounded the alarm, but they were too late. The wasps did not slow or change their course. They flew directly into the side of the mound, hitting with a sharp staccato of *thwumps*. The impacts killed a few hundred Alpha Zee citizens and woke thousands more. Groggy citizens were just beginning to ask each other what had happened when one of the *Camponotus* ants clenched his abdomen and erupted with thunderous force. Twenty-four floors on the west side of the mound collapsed. A second explosion ripped through the colony, followed, almost simultaneously, by four more.

Ground troops made their way to the surface as fast as they could and secured all the entrances that had not been destroyed. Winged forces took to the air in a swarming patrol. Citizens cowered in their chambers. The Queen and several virgin females crept into a special, secure chamber.

"Who did this?" President Kadira growled, staring at each of his three Secretaries in turn. They averted their eyes and stood completely still, as if their lack of movement would make them invisible.

"We believe—" the Secretary of Defense began.

"You believe *what*?" the President spat.

"That it might be—"

"—someone we know," the Secretaries of State and Homeland Security said cryptically.

"What the hell are you talking about?" the President asked, scowling even more aggressively.

"Do you remember a wasp named Yasura Hasan?" the Secretary of Defense asked.

"We inserted her into Antistan to launch a civil war," the Secretary of State clarified.

"And we've helped her get into a few other colonies," the Secretary of Homeland Security added quietly.

"Yes, yes, yes, I remember her," the President said impatiently. He was unsettled by the fact that the Secretaries were speaking independently and in complete sentences.

"Well, it seems that she's laid quite a few eggs," the Secretary of State said.

"A *lot* of eggs," the Secretary of Defense confirmed.

"She's created quite a few wasp hatcheries," the Secretary of Homeland Security said.

"So Yasura Hasan attacked us?" the President asked, trying to piece together the information.

"Not her specifically," the Secretary of Defense said.

"She's actually pretty loyal to us," the Secretary of State said.

"But the wasps who attacked us were black with thin red lines down their flanks," the Secretary of Homeland Security said.

"They were Hasan's progeny," the Secretary of Defense confirmed.

"We don't have much control over them," the Secretary of State said.

"They hate us," the Secretary of Homeland Security said.

The President asked, "Exactly how many colonies have we helped Hasan infiltrate?"

"Ah," the Secretary of Defense said quickly, "we probably shouldn't talk in specific numbers, Mr. President."

"It's really not instructive to try to hone in on an exact figure," the Secretary of State agreed.

"We helped her get into ... a few," the Secretary of Homeland Security said. "I think *a few* is the phrase we're looking for." The three Secretaries nodded in unison.

"And now her *off-spring* have turned against us?" President Kadira asked incredulously.

"'Turned against us' isn't quite accurate," the Secretary of State said.

"They were never really *with us* in the first place," the Secretary of Defense said.

"Their existence was simply a by-product of our relationship with Hasan."

"And they—"

"—hate—"

"—us," the Secretaries said.

"But we helped give them life," the President complained.

"They also believe—"

"—quite irrationally—"

"—that we've made their lives worse," the Secretaries said.

"Those ungrateful little—," the President started.

"We—"

"—should—"

"—kill them!" the Secretaries said.

"Where do they live?" the President asked.

As if on cue, Ambassador Lucas Mallen stepped out of the shadows and said, "Some of them live in the very colony that is now threatening our fungus supply."

"Antistan!" the President said. The Secretaries smiled ominously.

twenty-eight

The day after the terrorist attacks, Alpha Zee President Kadira strode out onto his platform. His steely eyes glinted with rage, and his mandibles jutted out in a determined set. He stared out at the assembled throng; their stunned faces and fear-widened eyes were raised to him expectantly.

"We are freedom lovers!" he said.

"Freedom lovers," the citizens repeated, but without their usual vigor. Their voices were choked and confused; the hollow sound barely echoed off the walls.

"We are peace lovers!" President Kadira insisted, hoping that his confidence would be infectious.

"Peace Lovers!" the residents of Alpha Zee said with a little more passion.

"Yesterday, *cowards* attacked us." Ambassador Mallen had suggested that he use the word *coward* early and often.

"COWARDS!" the crowd agreed, almost at full volume.

"Thousands of innocent ants were killed."

"INNOCENTS!" the citizens cried.

"We know who did this," President Kadira said.

The crowd fell silent. They'd spent an entire day and night scared and agitated, ignorant about *who* could have committed such a horrible assault on their home. The Alpha Zee Colony was the greatest democracy ever known. It had opened its arms to ants of dozens of different species—not creating slaves, but actually granting full citizenship to aliens and allowing the Queen to mate with other species so that she could create hybrids. Why would someone do this to them?

"The wasp who masterminded this attack has perpetrated acts of terrorism all over The Great Plain," President Kadira continued. "Her name is Yasura Hasan. We've had our eye on her for a long time. We've tried to take her out covertly on numerous occasions, but she has used her terror network to stay clear of our grasp. This wasp has sparked civil wars in dozens of colonies. She's used chemical and biological weapons. She's caused massive bloodshed. And now she's made the fatal mistake of attacking us!"

"*FATAL* MISTAKE!"

"We will not be intimidated by terrorists! We will seek vengeance!"

"VENGEANCE!"

"And we know where they are."

The crowd grew still. If the President knew where the terrorists were located, then the powerful Alpha Zee military would soon be exacting revenge for this horrific attack.

"Antistan," President Kadira said.

"Antistan?" the crowd asked uncertainly.

"Antistan!" the President said again.

"ANTISTAN!"

"I have a special guest today. He's our Ambassador to Antistan, and he's done courageous work down there. Ambassador Lucas Mallen, come on out here!"

Ambassador Mallen waddled out onto the platform and the crowd applauded politely. Although he had been one of the most famous and powerful ants in the Alpha Zee Colony since his birth, he'd been living in Antistan for so long that many ants had never seen him, and those who had, didn't really remember him. They didn't know what to make of this obese ant with no mandibles.

General Ainsley Walters watched from his chamber, high up the wall opposite the platform. He was curious to hear how the President, the Ambassador, and the Secretaries would pin the blame on Yasura Hasan without implicating themselves for helping the wasp when it served their needs.

"Ambassador Mallen," the President said, "I want you to tell the citizens of Alpha Zee what you've learned about Antistan during your long tour of duty."

"Thank you, Mr. President. Well, first of all," he said to the crowd, "I must emphasize that there are many good citizens in Antistan. Many dedicated workers and caretakers who just want to put in a hard day's labor and raise their young."

The crowd nodded. The citizens of Alpha Zee didn't doubt that a few good ants could be found even in a place as horrible as Antistan.

"The problem," Ambassador Mallen said, "is that a relatively small group of insurgents has gained control of the colony. They oppose democracy and free trade, and their actions have turned the hive into a terrorist breeding ground for wasps like Yasura Hasan and her offspring. The leader is a worker named Ashanti Lehana, and for the past few months she's risen to power using all manner of manipulations and intimidations." Ambassador Mallen had to raise his voice to be heard over the buzz of the angry crowd.

General Ainsley Waters leaped to his feet, shocked to learn that Ashanti had taken control of the government.

"Months ago, Ashanti burst into President Paulo Gamba's office and threatened physical violence. When that approach failed to accomplish her goals, she incited the workers to slow their production in hopes of hurting Alpha Zee's access to the fungus that we need to feed our Queen and our pupae and our military," Ambassador Mallen said. "She openly challenged President Gamba during his daily orations and then organized an illegal election, which resulted in her being chosen as the new President. Among her campaign promises was a vow to completely cut off the fungus that is shipped here to Alpha Zee."

The crowd moaned. This scared them even more than the terrorist attacks. How could an ant be so indifferent to the suffering she would cause if she followed through with this diabolical plan? Fungus was the Alpha Zee's most precious import, and nearly 90 percent of it came from Antistan. The Alpha Zee way of life would collapse if Lehana cut off the fungus supply.

General Walters stood with his mouth agape, barely able to believe the lies and half-truths he was hearing.

"Even though the rigged election had no legitimate authority," Ambassador Mallen continued, "President Gamba recognized that the workers needed representation in the government, so he generously offered to make Ashanti Lehana his Vice President and put her in charge of worker relations. She rejected this offer, because she wanted total control."

The crowd muttered angrily.

"A day after the election," Ambassador Mallen said, "President Gamba tried to congratulate Ashanti Lehana and welcome her to his government, but the crowd wouldn't permit him to speak. They drowned out their legitimate President with jeers, and he could do nothing but back away from the platform. When Ashanti took the stage, they chanted her name for nearly five minutes." Ambassador Mallen paused and looked over the audience with a pained expression as if he wished he didn't have to have to tell them these terrible facts. "This is not a government they've elected down there; it's a religion. They're worshiping an individual—and a very dangerous individual at that. Ashanti Lehana has no political experience, no interest in free trade, and no sense of fairness. I've offered to serve as her mentor, but she has refused my help. The terrorist attack that we suffered here in Alpha Zee was the result of her incompetent leadership. Terrorists roam freely in Antistan, and unless we do something, they will strike again."

The crowd was ready to do whatever needed to be done to force Ashanti Lehana out of power.

Ambassador Mallen shook his head wearily. "I pleaded with her to be a partner in the peace process. I asked her what she planned to do in response to our good will in recent months and she said,"—he consulted a scrap of paper—"and I'm quoting. She said, 'I completely reject any suggestion that the Alpha Zee has treated us with good will.'"

The crowd was shocked by this repudiation. How could she say that after everything Alpha Zee had done to help her and her fellow citizens with honeydew during their time of need?

"She said that she didn't have an immediate plan to attack us, but if she *did* attack she says that she'd be 'more than justified.'"

The crowd shuddered.

"Thank you, Ambassador Mallen," President Kadira said. He looked out over the crowd. "We will not allow this threat to blossom in our backyard. We will institute immediate unilateral sanctions against Antistan, which we hope will pressure Ashanti Lehana to surrender. But if she does not, we'll be forced to send troops after her. How this will end is up to her. We'll take her peacefully, or by force, but make no mistake—"

"MAKE NO MISTAKE!"

"—the outcome is certain."

"CERTAIN!"
"Because we are freedom lovers!"
"FREEDOM LOVERS!"
"Peace lovers!"
"PEACE LOVERS!"
"And those who threaten our freedom must be destroyed!"
"DESTROYED!"

twenty-nine

General Ainsley Walters smashed a fist into the wall and called Ashanti's name over and over. Why hadn't he stayed in Anti-stan to guide her? Why hadn't he dragged her away to some far away spot where they could spend the rest of their lives together? Why had he returned to this cell where he could do nothing but listen impotently as the colony made plans to kill the only ant he'd ever loved?

Sulaiman Solidarius stood across the room, watching his inmate carefully. "General . . .," Sulaiman asked carefully. "Are you okay?"

General Walters turned away from the wall and looked at Sulaiman with a tear-streaked face. He was not ashamed of his emotions. He felt shame only for failing to protect Ashanti.

"I have to get down there," General Walters said, solemnly.

"I ... I can't let you do that," Sulaiman stammered.

"You listened to that speech," General Walters said, pointing toward the main chamber. "You heard the lies they told about her!"

Sulaiman shook his head. "You can't expect me to believe that the President and the Ambassador lied to us."

General Walters hung his head. "Sulaiman, I'm going to tell you something that you may find hard to believe, but if you pay attention, you'll understand."

Sulaiman Solidarius nodded slowly and waited.

"The most powerful politicians," General Walters began, "have a unique skill. They can lie and tell the truth at the same time."

Sulaiman scowled doubtfully, waiting for a punch line. "That hardly seems possible. Either you're telling the truth or you're lying."

General Walters had never experienced emotions like those that were flooding his body at the moment. He was terrified about what the Alpha Zee military might do to Ashanti. "Everything they just said about Ashanti was the truth. She *did* barge into the President's office; she *was* prepared to fight him; she *did* organize a work slowdown; she *did* try to hurt Alpha Zee's fungus supply; she *did* organize an election; the ants there *did* vote for her; and although I wasn't there to see it, I have no doubt that she *did* terminate Alpha Zee's contracts. And, yes, there *are* terrorists roaming freely in Antistan."

"So they told the truth," Sulaiman said.

"Yes, but they were lying too," General Walters said.

Sulaiman scowled again. "That doesn't make any sense."

"When you tell a story about someone you can make him or her sound like a good ant or an evil ant, depending on how you present the details," General Walters said. "So I'm going to tell you a story about Ashanti Lehana, and I'm going to use the same basic facts that Ambassador Mallen used."

"Okay," Sulaiman said.

"Nearly two years ago, the Alpha Zee Senate concluded that we needed a steady supply of the nutritious fungus that Antistan produces, but our attempts to negotiate with them failed because we had nothing of value to offer, and they were not intimidated by our threats. And the problem was that we simply couldn't overrun them and take the fungus. We had to find a way to subjugate them so that they would keep producing fungus, and we could keep receiving it. So Lucas Mallen devised a scheme. Our military helped a wasp named Yasura Hasan infiltrate the mound to spark a pseudo-civil war, which caused enough injury to Antistan's military for us to launch a coup that put Paulo Gamba in power. He promptly sold his citizens into slavery, *giving* the Alpha Zee a huge portion of the fungus that the workers of Antistan had labored so hard to produce.

"Ashanti was just a citizen concerned about her hive, so she went to the President's quarters to talk to him. Ambassador Mallen and I were there, and Gamba snapped. He flew into a rage and tried to kill her.

"But rather than retreating, Ashanti stood her ground. She did not attack, let alone try to kill the President. But she was prepared to defend herself. I intervened and she escaped.

"Later, she decided that the only way she could save most of her brothers and sisters from slavery and starvation was by convincing them to slow down their production. Even though hundreds of thousands of her brothers and sisters died, the others continued to work slower and produce less food. Then she learned that we had deliberately bombed their medicinal warehouses to cause additional suffering and deaths."

"Then Ashanti discovered that Gamba had sold the rights to one of their foraging areas to us without the citizens' knowledge and had further decreased their rations.

"The citizens demanded an election, and they freely chose Ashanti Lehana as their new President, because she was the only ant who has demonstrated enough intellect and initiative to run the government. The lesson of this story is that Ashanti Lehana is a true patriot. She has shown great courage and ingenuity in fighting for the freedom and well-being of her citizens."

General Walters stopped and looked expectantly at Sulaiman.

Sulaiman shook his head. "You manipulated the facts to make her sound like something she isn't."

"I simply told you more of the facts—facts that President Kadira and Ambassador Mallen intentionally omitted. But what I'm trying to explain is that no one can know the whole truth, no matter how hard he tries. Each of us unconsciously filters what we hear and see. But some ants consciously lie— they intentionally withhold some of the facts or make up information to distort the truth," General Walters said. "I'm just telling you what I *understand* to be the truth. I am not intentionally lying."

"But you think the President and the Ambassador were intentionally lying."

"I *know* that they are."

"Why would the President lie to us?"

"Sulaiman, I think the President and his Secretaries have lost their way. We are no longer fit for a nomadic existence. We've become so dependent on fungus that our leaders are willing to do just about anything to ensure our access to it. It doesn't matter how many innocent ants suffer or die in the process."

"So what *is* the truth?" Sulaiman asked.

"In this case, the truth is that the Alpha Zee military will kill Ashanti Lehana and many other innocent citizens if I don't get down there to talk to her."

Sulaiman stared at the General for a long moment. Finally he said, "General, I believe that your intentions are noble, and I believe that you are telling the truth. I will help you escape."

General Walters stepped forward and gave Sulaiman a fatherly hug. "I appreciate your belief in me, but I can't let you get in trouble." Walters reared back and used the blunt side of his mandibles to hit Sulaiman in the head. The hybrid groaned and slumped to the ground unconscious. "I'm sorry," General Walters said to Sulaiman's prone body. "But that's for your own protection."

thirty

General Ainsley Walters ran non-stop from Alpha Zee to Antistan. When he finally arrived, he was breathless but energized. *God, it felt good to be free!* The Alpha Zee military would set up its blockade within days, so if Ashanti was going to escape, she would have to leave immediately.

Walters raced through the dilapidated corridors of the mound and burst into the Presidential chamber. "Ashanti!" he shouted, but his voice echoed in the empty space.

He turned back into the hallway and called her name. Several workers from nearby chambers watched him carefully. They could tell by his scent that he was an Alpha Zee soldier, and they were intimidated by his size. But they also somehow sensed that he was not a threat to them.

"Where can I find Ashanti Lehana?" the General asked.

"You're General Walters!" one of the workers beamed.

"*The* General Walters," another worker said, smiling broadly.

The workers broke into a chant. "*ALLY* FOR ANTISTAN! *ALLY* FOR ANTISTAN!"

General Walters smiled in confusion. How did these ants know who he was and that he was a friend? They chanted happily as they led General Walters down the hallway. More citizens came out of their chambers as the phalanx passed through the convoluted passageways. The chanting grew louder.

"*ALLY* FOR ANTISTAN! *ALLY* FOR ANTISTAN!"

Ashanti heard them coming from a long way off and raced toward the sound. She came around a bend in the corridor and stopped when she saw the General's huge frame stooped to negotiate the small tunnel.

"I see you've met my family," she said, rushing forward to give him a tight embrace.

General Walters smiled and squeezed her tightly.

"*ALLY* FOR ANTISTAN! *ALLY* FOR ANTISTAN!" The crowd cheered.

"I don't understand how they know me," the General said, laughing.

"I told them how you saved me in President Gamba's chamber. It's been rough for us for a long time, and it gave us great comfort to know that we had such a highly placed ally in the Alpha Zee power structure."

"I need to talk to you privately," General Walters said.

"Come on in," she said, leading him back down the hallway to her tiny quarters. The massive general barely fit through her door and decided to sit down rather than stand hunched over.

"You have to escape," General Walters said without preamble.

Ashanti stroked his face with her mandibles.

He rubbed her face, too, marveling at how good it felt to be with her. "I'm serious, Ashanti. The Alpha Zee military will be here tomorrow. They're going to blockade your mound, and they will kill you."

"I'm just one ant," Ashanti said peacefully. "It doesn't matter if they kill me."

General Walters paused. "But if something happens to you, who will lead Antistan?"

"Excuse me for a moment." She squeezed past him and walked out into the hallway, where her brothers and sisters were still gathered.

"If something happens to me," she yelled, "who will lead our tribe?"

"WE WILL!"

"What will you do?" Ashanti asked.

"WE'LL HOLD AN ELECTION!" They chanted. "WE'LL CHOOSE A NEW PRESIDENT."

"And what if something happens to that President?"

"WE'LL HOLD ANOTHER ELECTION! WE'LL CHOOSE ANOTHER PRESIDENT!"

Ashanti turned back to General Walters. "I'm just one ant. This hive is much bigger than me."

General Walters studied Ashanti admiringly. He didn't know how she had developed these ideas or how she understood so much about business and politics, but a surge of hope coursed through him as he realized that simple workers could gain such insights on their own.

"Come back inside," he said. "We need to talk."

They sat on the floor of her chamber, rubbing each other's heads as they talked about everything that had happened since they'd last seen each other.

"What you've done here is the most impressive thing I've ever seen," General Walters said eventually.

Ashanti shrugged off the compliment.

"I'm serious," General Walters continued. "You've grasped concepts that even well-traveled and well-studied ants don't understand. And even now, you're atypical. One of the paradoxes of democracy is that ants tend to believe in the value of shared power right up until the moment that they gain power. Then they do everything that they can to stay on top, even if that means breaking the principles that they profess to believe in. But even as you sit in the presidency, you're still teaching your citizens that they should be prepared for life after you're gone."

Ashanti blushed.

"But here's what you have to think about," General Walters said. "The Alpha Zee military isn't going to come here with a small strike force to kill you. They're going to send a full battalion to initiate sanctions against Antistan. They're going to cut off your food, water and medical supplies. They're not going to let your foragers go out and gather leaves. Nothing will get in or out, and they're going to bomb any part of the mound that seems threatening to them."

Ashanti watched the General carefully, and he could tell by her expression that she hadn't considered this possibility, but she quickly figured it out.

"My only choice is to surrender."

General Walters exhaled loudly, "Even if you surrender, they'll kill you."

"But maybe they won't impose sanctions on the hive."

"They probably will, at least temporarily, to make sure everyone understands who is in control."

"Will I get a trial?"

"Yes," General Walters said slowly, "but it will be in front of a military tribunal, and your guilt will be guaranteed before any evidence is presented."

Ashanti nodded solemnly. "Will other colonies on The Great Plain know that I've been captured, tried and executed?"

General Walters said, "Yes, the Alpha Zee government would declare far and wide that they'd captured the alleged dictator who turned Antistan into a haven for terrorists.

"Then, I will surrender," Ashanti said. "And I have an idea." She squeezed past the General again, and stepped out into the hallway. "My brothers and sisters, please tell everyone to gather in The Great Chamber in fifteen minutes. I have an important announcement to make."

A short time later, she stood on the high Presidential platform and told her citizens that the Alpha Zee military would soon arrive to form a blockade around their mound, and once they did, Ashanti was prepared to surrender herself.

"But I am not surrendering the mound!" she proclaimed. "I'm merely giving them *me*, because they say they want me."

The crowd groaned, but she continued.

"I have a suggestion, and I want all of you to think about it carefully, and then cast your votes within the next few hours," Ashanti said. "You've elected me and 100 Senators to lead this colony. After I leave, you'll need to choose a new President. But the moment that I'm out of power, Alpha Zee will try to install a new President—probably Paulo Gamba again."

The crowd booed. "GAMBA MUST GO!" They chanted.

"That's right," Ashanti said. "Don't accept him as your President. If he tries to deliver a speech, do what you did the last time and drown him out. But here's my suggestion: In the event of an emergency, we need a process that will give us an automatic interim President until you can elect a new one. You could prioritize your 100 Senators, so that one of them would become the President if something happened to me, and then another one would become President if something happened to the ant who replaced me, and so on."

The crowd seemed to mull over this idea.

"The reason I suggest this," Ashanti continued, "is that we're fighting to have a democratically elected government here, and Alpha Zee won't let us. If they want to arrest me and sentence me to death, then I'll let them. But I know that one of our Senators will immediately fill the presidency. And if they want to arrest and kill that ant, then he or she should sur-render and let the next Senator fill the void. And so on. We've always been ready to sacrifice our lives for the colony. Now we can do it for the right to be free to govern ourselves." Ashanti paused and turned to General Walters. "We'll see how long the other tribes of The Great Plain will stand by as leader after leader is arrested and executed by the Alpha Zee."

"LIVE FREE OR *DIE!*" the ants exclaimed.

General Walters nodded his approval, once again impressed by Ashanti's ingenuity.

thirty-one

Ashanti, General Walters, and thousands of workers walked through the mound together, heading to the west, where the Alpha Zee command center was located. As they approached the edge of the mound, a small translucent ant crept out of a side corridor.

"Excuse me," the little ant said.

Ashanti and General Walters stopped and stared, not quite sure of what they were seeing.

"Are you leaving?" the little ant asked. She was so frail that even the effort of talking seemed to be too much strain for her.

"Yes," Ashanti said.

"Can you take me with you?"

Ashanti wasn't sure this little ant would want a ride when she learned the destination. "Who are you?"

"My name is Hasina Binsaw," she said. "I've been living with your Queen since the last civil war. I'm a parasite." Hasina considered herself lucky to be alive. Most of her offspring had died of malnutrition and disease.

"How did you get here?" General Walters asked.

"The Alpha Zee brought me in."

"Why?" Ashanti asked.

"They wanted me to keep Ambassador Mallen informed about the Queen's birthing percentages."

General Walters marveled at the brilliance of this strategy. Hasina had been a well-placed spy; she had provided the information that allowed Ambassador Mallen to control the size of the Antistani military.

"*Please* take me with you," Hasina said.

"We're not going to help you leech off another hive," General Walters said. He started walking again.

"I won't lay any eggs!" Hasina promised desperately. "All I need is a home for myself. Please, don't leave me here!"

General Walters sighed. He picked up Hasina and threw her onto his back. "I'll take you back to Alpha Zee with me," he said, "but only *you*. You can't lay any eggs. After that, you can hitch a ride to a termite mound."

"Thank you!" Hasina said, holding on tightly as General Walters marched forward.

When they reached the edge of the Antistani mound, they could see that Alpha Zee soldiers were lined up half a coron away. Ashanti turned to her brothers and sisters and told them to stay back. She and General Walters—with Hasina on his back—walked forward slowly. Hasina crouched down and mimicked General Walters' scent. The soldiers would never know that she was there.

When they reached the line of soldiers, Ashanti asked, "Who is in charge?"

"Who are you?" one of the soldiers asked.

"I'm Ashanti Lehana, President of Antistan and I wish to surrender.

"Wait here," the soldier said. He turned and raced into the underbrush. A short time later, a large Alpha Zee general marched out toward her.

"You had enough?" General Edmund Gant sneered. Then he paused, "General Walters? What are you doing here?"

"Advising Ashanti," General Walters said.

Ambassador Lucas Mallen stepped out of the underbrush, smirking.

"Hello, General Walters. I would say it's a surprise to see you, but knowing your traitorous tendencies, it's not." His laughter hid a nervous twitch. He'd come down to watch the commencement of the blockade and planned to return to Alpha Zee to wait things out. The workers of Antistan had maintained the work slowdown for months, so he expected the embargo to stretch on for a while.

"So what's on your mind, Ashanti," the Ambassador asked.

"I want to surrender," she said.

"That scared, huh?" Ambassador Mallen smiled, but he was starting to sweat. Ashanti's surrender was never part of his plan.

"I'm not afraid," Ashanti said. "I'm looking forward to having a trial—even if it's a sham."

Ambassador Mallen's mind was racing. He'd had a long talk with President Kadira and the Secretaries, and the consensus was that the last thing the Alpha Zee wanted to do was *capture* Ashanti Lehana and put her on trial. They'd prefer that she starve to death or get killed by a bomb.

"Well, we're not yet ready to take any prisoners," Ambassador Mallen said, confusing everyone.

General Walters waited a moment and then asked, "When will you be ready?"

"In a few days," Ambassador Mallen said, starting to turn away. He needed to go back to Alpha Zee and consult with the President.

"Well, I'm ready to surrender," Ashanti insisted.

Ambassador Mallen was sweating in earnest now. He turned and glared at Ashanti, not quite believing that this little worker had foiled him at every turn. Now she wanted to embarrass Alpha Zee by surrendering before the blockade had even begun in earnest. Ambassador Mallen knew that his only hope was to goad Ashanti into losing her composure.

"Why don't you just go back inside!" he said. His obese body lunged forward faster than anyone could have imagined, and he shoved her hard.

"Hey!" Ashanti said.

Thousands of Antistani workers charged toward the perimeter. The Alpha Zee soldiers responded by clapping their mandibles.

Ambassador Mallen pushed Ashanti again, and General Ainsley Walters, who'd been caught off guard the first time, didn't hesitate the second time. He reached over and sliced clean through the Ambassador's neck.

"Let me go!" Ambassador Mallen's disembodied head demanded, not yet realizing that it didn't have a body. "Let me—" he managed again, before his eyes rolled back in his head and blood gurgled out of his mouth.

Antistani citizens continued to surge forward.

"Stay back!" Ashanti cautioned. But her brothers and sisters didn't hear her, and she didn't get a chance to repeat her admonition—four Alpha Zee soldiers grabbed her.

"No!" General Walters screamed! He moved toward her, but another group of soldiers held him back. "No!" he cried again, watching helplessly as Alpha Zee soldiers tore Ashanti limb from limb.

As Ashanti's lifeless body fell to the ground, Justine stepped forward and said proudly, "I am the new President of Antistan, and I would like to surrender."

thirty-two

General Edmund Gant and a platoon of soldiers escorted General Ainsley Walters back to the Alpha Zee hive, and marched him straight into President Kadira's private chamber. The President was huddled with his three Secretaries, discussing the tragic death of Ambassador Mallen. They weren't sure how they would make foreign policy decisions without his guidance. The President pointed an antennae at General Walters, and said, "What's *he* doing here?"

"We captured him *in* Antistan," General Gant sneered proudly. General Walters stood with his head down, resigned to his fate. Now that Ashanti was dead, he could think of no reason to continue living.

"*Captured?*" The Secretary of State asked.

"Why not—"

"—*killed?*" the Secretaries of defense and homeland security finished.

"Why in the hell would you bring him back *here?*" President Kadira demanded.

"I thought—" General Gant stuttered.

"You're not paid to think, soldier!" President Kadira stormed. "Get him out of here! Get him out of Alpha Zee!"

"Where should we—"

"It doesn't matter where!" the Secretary of State said.

"You shouldn't have brought him *here*, you idiot!" the Secretary of Defense said.

"Get rid of him!" The Secretary of Homeland Security said.

The soldiers were backing out of the chamber when Sulaiman Solidarius and two dozen hybrids arrived. Sulaiman looked relieved to see General Walters, as if he'd expected to arrive too late. He turned to the President and said, "The Queen has requested a meeting with General Walters."

"How does she even know that he's here?" President Kadira asked, his mind racing. Sulaiman bore the royal pheromone, so there was no question that he'd just come from the Queen. But the President couldn't let General Walters talk to her. The General knew too much.

"The Queen is well-informed," Sulaiman said, staring at President Kadira without the slightest hint of nervousness. The hybrid exuded the chemical of justice, and he wouldn't let anything—not even his President—stand in the way of performing his duties.

"Tell her that we can't release the General until he's been debriefed," the President suggested. "We'll send him down as soon as we're done."

"That's standard operating procedure—"

"—when we capture one of our own—"

"—aiding and abetting the enemy," the Secretaries explained.

Sulaiman shook his head. "She wants to see him immediately."

The President studied the situation. The soldiers standing in the hallway easily outnumbered the hybrids who had come to retrieve General Walters. The soldiers could kill the hybrids and the General and drag all of their bodies out of the mound.

President Kadira glanced at the Secretaries, and his murderous thoughts must have been emblazoned on his face, because the Secretaries frowned and shook their heads almost imperceptibly, silently telling the President that the soldiers wouldn't obey that command. They'd already taken General Walters as a prisoner rather than killing him in Antistan. Their loyalty toward him would not be easily broken.

Sulaiman took the President's silence as acquiescence, and he guided General Walters out of the chamber. The soldiers parted slowly to allow the hybrids to pass. President Kadira's mind raced through the possibilities, but without Lucas Mallen's guidance, he simply didn't know what to do.

After the General and the hybrids had departed, the Secretaries huddled close to the President.

"Perhaps now would be a good time to tell you—" the Secretary of State whispered.

"—that the wasp Yasura Hasan is nearby," the Secretary of Defense continued.

"She's been living camouflaged in Anterbijan for the past year," the Secretary of Homeland Security said.

"Then why haven't we killed her?" the President asked incredulously.

"She could help us get rid of the hybrids—"

"—and General Walters—"

"—all at the same time," the Secretaries said.

President Kadira hesitated for a brief moment and then said, "How soon could she be here?"

thirty-three

Sulaiman Solidarius walked next to General Walters with his head held high and his chest forward. Queen Wenonah had summoned him, and he was still savoring the sweet fragrance of her instructions.

Bring the General to me, and do not let anyone stop you, the Queen had whispered. *I trust you with this task, because you and the other hybrids are uniquely qualified to serve the interests of justice. The President will try to kill General Walters. We cannot let that happen.*

General Walters felt numb as he descended into the deepest chambers of the mound. Although he was eager to see his Queen, he knew that whatever she had planned for him was futile. She might be able to save his life for the moment, but he would be dead within the week.

The Queen's heavily guarded chamber was filled with pungent pheromones that washed over her citizens and imbued them with a sense of well-being. Every few seconds, a caretaker stepped forward to receive a new egg, which the Queen effortlessly expelled from her gaster.

Please come closer, Queen Wenonah said to General Walters with a gentle scent that easily cut through the thick soup of pheromones. As the General stepped forward, the Queen smiled at Sulaiman. *Thank you for following my instructions to the letter.*

"You're welcome, Majesty," Sulaiman said softly.

General Walters stood in front of Queen Wenonah, and she wrapped her antennae tightly around his, pulling him in to have a private scent conversation.

It's good to see you again, she said. They were face-to-face, and the gentle vibration of her antennae sent a shiver through General Walters. In this position the General didn't need to speak. All he had to do was think his words and the Queen would hear them.

Thank you, Majesty. It's good to see you, too.

Is it true that you've become a terrorist sympathizer? She asked the question with gentle mockery. Walters could see in her eyes that she didn't believe it.

I met a young ant named Ashanti Lehana who restored my faith in miracles.

Now she's dead?

Yes, Majesty.

And you plan to join her by getting yourself executed.

General Walters shrugged. *Probably.*

The Queen nodded soberly. *The President, the Secretaries, and the Senate believe that I'm ignorant about life on the surface. They believe that I obey their scent decrees without question. But, actually, I know everything that happens in and around our colony. I have many watchers who give me daily reports. I know that you are not a traitor.*

Thank you, Majesty.

You could prove that to your fellow citizens in a public trial.

I won't get a public trial. I'm a soldier. The President will convene a military tribunal, and I'll be prosecuted in a secret proceeding.

Then you must escape. It's already arranged. Just after sundown, the hybrids that brought you down here, will remove you from the jail and escort you out of the hive. I will soak them in a special royal guardian pheromone, so that no one will stop them. I've sent word to the Queen of Antgola and she will give you and the hybrids safe harbor.

I can't escape, Majesty.

Of course you can. You've done it twice. This time, you won't return.

General Walters shook his head. *Majesty, I escaped previously because I needed to help Ashanti Lehana. In some ways she was young and naïve and in need of my guidance, but in other ways, she was the wisest ant I've ever met. She would not flee from her own certain death, and neither will I.*

But you are among the wisest ants that I know, Queen Wenonah pleaded. *We can't lose you. We need your clear thinking and your willingness to disobey unjust orders. We need you to be a role model for younger ants. I've been laying more hybrid eggs every day. Currently, nearly a third of our population is composed of hybrids. If you can't live here in Alpha Zee, you must live somewhere else, because we will soon need you back to help lead our colony.*

General Walters thought for a long moment. *After our soldiers assassinated Ashanti, one of her sisters stepped forward and said, 'I'm the new President of Antistan, and I would like to surrender.' The soldiers killed her too, and another sister stepped forward and said, 'I am the new President of Antistan, and I would like to surrender.' The soldiers killed her. The executions continued in this fashion until our troops had assassinated more than twenty Antistani presidents. No one had prepared the soldiers to deal with a succession of presidential surrenders. At first they had simply followed their orders, but ultimately, some instinct for justice compelled them to stop. They realized that they couldn't follow their orders and stay on the path of justice at the same time. So they stopped killing Antistan's presidents. Watching them reach this realization was one of the proudest moments of my life.*

Queen Wenonah said, *When I hear these insights, I'm even more convinced that you must be saved.*

Suddenly, a clamor arose at the entrance of the royal chamber. The soldiers outside screamed, and the scent of panic flooded into the room just before a huge wasp stepped through the doorway.

General Walters tried to tear away from the Queen to launch himself at the terrorist, but Queen Wenonah released a pheromone that paralyzed the General.

Relax, she said. *I will handle this.*

The wasp pumped out a powerful chemical that filled the room with an acrid odor that normally would have plunged the ants into a pseudo civil war, but the hybrids were immune to the pheromone. They raced forward and latched onto the wasp. Yasura desperately dispersed even more chemicals, but the ants simply held her steady while one hybrid grabbed her stinger and ripped it from her body, taking her scent glands with it. Yasura screamed in agony, and slumped to the ground, disarmed and helpless.

I knew this day would come, Queen Wenonah said to the General, *so I have been breeding hybrids who would not be affected by the chemical manipulations of wasps.*

General Walters marveled at his Supreme Mother. *Then you must know that this wasp was sent here by the President and his Secretaries.*

We should let them believe that their plan has succeeded, Queen Wenonah said with a sly smile.

thirty-four

President Alexander Kadira strode out onto his high platform and surveyed his citizens, wondering how they would react to the dire news that he was about to share. Early that morning, the President had sent a scout to the royal chamber to check on the Queen. The panicked scout had raced back to the President and reported that everyone was gone—the Queen, her caretakers, the hybrids, and General Walters had all disappeared. The royal chamber was empty except for a swirling mass of pheromones that proved that enemy soldiers had somehow sneaked down to the hive's most heavily guarded room. The Queen and all of her attendants were presumed dead.

"Citizens," the President began, somberly, "I come to you today with a very heavy heart." President Kadira hadn't expected the wasp's pseudo civil war to lead to the Queen's death, but her departure was a blessing. Now he and the Secretaries could start fresh with a new Queen, over whom they would have much more control. "We have just learned that a wasp infiltrated our colony last night."

The crowd gasped.

"Using scent camouflage provided by General Walters and a platoon of hybrids, the wasp made it all the way down to the Queen's chamber before our soldiers finally detected the infiltrator."

The crowd listened in rapt silence.

"During the fight," the President said slowly, "the Queen was killed."

A visible shudder rippled through the audience, and President Kadira put up his forelegs, asking for silence. "There is no need to panic," he said. "The Secretaries and I have been working on a plan to help one of the princesses assume the throne."

Suddenly, a powerful scent question washed over the chamber.

Why don't you tell your citizens how you've conspired with the wasp, Yasura Hasan, to infiltrate eight hives in and around The Grove. Tell them about your policies that have turned these colonies into protected breeding grounds for several generations of wasps.

"Who is that?" President Kadira demanded, searching the audience below him.

It's me, the voice said. Queen Wenonah stepped out of the shadows on a balcony opposite President Kadira. The crowd gasped and dropped to the ground respectfully. *Or has my scent become foreign to you since you sent a wasp to kill me?*

"What … what … are you talking about, Majesty?" President Kadira stammered. "I don't know where you're getting this information, but I can assure you that it's—"

I got my information from the wasp, Queen Wenonah said. Yasura Hasan stepped out of the shadows and stood next to the Queen. The wasp was still a large and imposing figure but without her stinger and scent gland, she was as docile as an aphid.

All of the color drained out of President Kadira's face. He turned to leave the platform and found his path blocked by General Walters, Sulaiman Solidarius and a platoon of hybrids.

"Get out of my way!" the President barked, but the General didn't budge and neither did the hybrids.

"Mr. President," General Walters said, "by order of the Senate, we've already taken the Secretaries into custody, and now you're under arrest on the charges of treason, and attempted assassination of the Queen."

"You won't take me alive," President Kadira said. He charged at General Walters, expecting the soldier to react instinctively and kill him, but the General calmly reached out and grabbed President Kadira by the neck.

"A quick death would be too easy for you," General Walters said. "You're going to get a fair trial."

"I don't want a trial!" the President screeched, flailing help-lessly in General Walter's grip.

"I bet you don't," General Walters said, carrying the President away from his high chamber.

Queen Wenonah sprayed a misty scent of assurance out over the crowd, letting them know that the President would soon face trial, and that everyone would have the opportu-nity to attend. In the meantime, they would prepare for an election. They needed a new President, and General Ainsley Walters would be among the candidates.

About the Author

Reggie Rivers is a former NFL running back who played six seasons with the Denver Broncos (1991-1996). Since his playing career, Reggie has been a mainstay in the Denver media, working as a general-topic talk radio host, writing opinion-editorial columns for the Denver Post, hosting the public affairs show, "Global Agenda," on PBS, serving as a sports anchor for CBS, and authoring five books. Reggie holds a BA in Journalism from Texas State University, and a Master's in Global Studies from the University of Denver.